Widow's Walk

The Spenser Novels

WIDOW'S WALK

Robert B. Parker

G. P. Putnam's Sons   New York

G. P. Putnam's Sons
Publishers Since 1838
a member of
Penguin Putnam Inc.
375 Hudson Street
New York, NY 10014

Library of Congress Cataloging-in-Publication Data

Parker, Robert B., date.
    Widow's walk / Robert B. Parker
        p.   cm.
    ISBN 0-399-14845-0
        1. Spenser (Fictitious character)—Fiction.   2. Private
investigators—Massachusetts—Boston—Fiction.
    3. Boston (Mass.)—Fiction.   I. Title.
PS3566.A686 W53   2002   2001048771
813'.54—dc21

Printed in the United States of America

10   9   8   7   6   5   4   3   2   1

This book is printed on acid-free paper. ∞

Book design by Julie Duquet

Joan, Dave, and Dan: the rest is decoration.

CHAPTER **ONE**

"I think she's probably guilty," Rita Fiore said to me.

We were in her office, high up, with a view of the harbor.

"And you're her lawyer," I said.

"Tells you about her case," Rita said. She sat on the edge of her desk in front of me, her thick red hair gleaming. She had on a black suit with a very short skirt. Rita knew her legs were good.

"But you'll represent her anyway."

"Like everyone else," Rita said, "she's entitled to the best defense she can get."

"Or afford," I said.

Rita smiled. "Or afford."

"She got money?"

"Oodles," Rita said.

"Last time I worked for you," I said, "I almost got killed."

"I know," Rita said. "We could give you hazardous-duty pay."

"It's all hazardous duty," I said. "Tell me about your client."

"Mary Smith."

"Mary Smith?"

"Honest to God," Rita said. "It's her real name. She was married to the victim, Nathan Smith. Her maiden name was Toricelli."

"She have oodles of money before she married him?" I said.

"No."

"Ah ha!"

"Ah ha?"

"It's an investigational term," I said. "That where the oodles come from?"

"Yes."

"They the same age?"

"He married her when she was twenty-three and he was fifty-one."

"Prior marriages?"

"None. For either."

"How old is she now?"

"Thirty."

Rita had her legs crossed. She bounced the top leg a little, looking at the point of her shoe. The shoe had a very high heel. It looked uncomfortable. But good.

"Anyone else in her life?"

Rita shook her head sadly. "God," she said. "You're a cynical bastard."

"Anyone?"

"Cops suspect her of an affair or two."

"With?"

Rita smiled. "You want them in chronological order?" she said. "Or alphabetically?"

"You can give me a list," I said. "What's the prosecution's case?"

"He was discovered naked in his bed with a hole in his head made by a forty-caliber slug."

"They find the bullet?"

"Yes. After it went through his head it tore through the mattress and lodged in the baseboard. Angle of the shot suggests that it was fired by someone in bed beside him."

"She have an alibi?"

"No. She says she was downstairs in the library watching television."

"She hear the shot?"

"No. Says the TV was on loud and her door was closed so as not to wake him up."

"So she found him that way when she went up to bed."

"Yes. They didn't share a bedroom, but she usually stopped in to say good night."

"Did he normally sleep naked?" I said.

"I don't know."

"Okay," I said. "She's a good candidate. But they got to have more than that to prosecute."

"They had a huge fight earlier in the evening. He actually slapped her."

"Witnesses?"

"Two dozen. It was a big cocktail party in Brookline."

"And I assume she's his heir," I said.

"Yes."

"And there's more," I said.

"Unfortunately, yes. Prosecution has a witness who says she tried to hire him to kill her husband."

"And he declined?"

"He says he did."

"He make a deal for his testimony?"

"Yes. They picked him up for something unrelated. He said if they could work something out, he could help them with this case."

"Which is a high profiler," I said.

"The Smiths first came to Boston on the *Mayflower*," Rita said.

"The *Mayflower* didn't come to Boston," I said.

"Well, they've been here a long time," Rita said.

"But the cops can't put her in the room when the gun went off," I said.

"No."

"No powder residue on her hands."

"No. But he did."

"Shot at close range," I said. "Put his hands up to try and stop the bullet?"

"That's the police theory."

"Everybody knows about powder residue anyway," I said. "She could have worn gloves."

"Police didn't find them."

"You can flush those latex jobs down the toilet like a condom."

"I've heard that can happen," Rita said.

"I'll bet you have," I said.

"I meant about the gloves," Rita said.

"Oh."

"There is probably more," Rita said. "But that's what I know they've got so far."

"You think they can convict her on that?" I said.

"Motive, and opportunity, prior solicitations to murder. Plus the jury won't like her."

"Because?"

"Because she's what my mother would have called cheap. She's too pretty, too made up, too blond, lot of attitude, drinks to excess, probably does dope, sleeps around."

"Sounds like a great date," I said.

"And her diction is bad," Rita said. "She sounds uneducated."

"Juries don't like that?"

"They are more inclined to think you're innocent if you sound like Barbara Walters," Rita said.

"You think Barbara would be a good date?"

"Oh, oink," Rita said.

"You think the prosecution knows stuff they haven't told you?" I said.

Rita had thick dark red hair which glinted in the sunlight that streamed through her big picture window.

"Maybe," she said.

"What about full disclosure?" I said.

"What about the Easter bunny?" Rita said. "You want to see what you can find out?"

"Sure."

CHAPTER TWO

I was in the office of the Homicide Commander.

"If she did it," I said, "wouldn't she work up a better alibi?"

"You met her?" Quirk said.

"Not yet."

"When you do, don't let her do brain surgery."

"Not smart?"

"Not even close," Quirk said.

"Maybe the alibi is elegant in its simplicity," I said.

"I know," Quirk said. "We thought about that. A lot of cases you got some rocket scientist who has six witnesses say that he was a hundred miles away, which gives you a place to start. All you got to do is poke a hole in one witness and the whole thing collapses."

"You can't disprove her alibi."

"Nope."

"And it occurs to a seasoned investigator like myself that only an innocent person would have an alibi that sucked this bad."

"Seasoned investigator," Quirk said.

"So maybe she's smarter than we think she is."

"Even if she were much smarter than we think she is . . ."

"She's not capable of trickery?"

"Talk to her," Quirk said. "And get back to me."

"You don't think it's a double fake," I said.

"She's dumber than my dick," Quirk said.

"That dumb?" I said.

"But better-looking," Quirk said.

"Anything you don't like about the case?" I said.

"I'd like to find the murder weapon. I'd like to tie her to it. I'd like to put her in the room when he died."

"And you'd like to have a video of her pulling the trigger."

"Yeah."

"That aside," I said, "anything that doesn't seem right to you?"

Quirk was a big strong healthy-looking guy, one of the two or three toughest people I'd ever met. He was also one of the most orderly. There was nothing in his office that didn't need to be there, and what was there was neatly arranged. The only thing on the desk was a plastic cube that displayed his wife and children and the family dog.

"Other than the lousy alibi? No."

"There were powder burns on his hands," I said.

"Sure. He shot himself then got rid of the gun so we wouldn't catch him."

"Maybe somebody wanted to cover up the suicide."

"Sure. Or maybe Dr. Kevorkian stopped by."

"Just a thought."

"Somebody points a gun at you," Quirk said, "close range, you put your hands up in front of your face like to protect yourself."

Quirk raised his hands.

"Guy pulls the trigger," he said. "You get powder residue on your hands."

"Good point," I said. "But wouldn't it be on the palms, where if he shot himself it would be on the back?"

"And if he shot himself it would be mostly on the gun hand," Quirk said.

"Yes."

"He had powder residue on both hands, mostly on the palms."

"I hate when you're right," I said.

"I'm used to it," Quirk said. "She did it. Go talk to her."

"You know anything I don't know?"

"A lot," Quirk said, "but not about this case."

"You think they'll convict her?"

"In a heartbeat," Quirk said. "Jury will hate her."

"That's pretty much what Rita said."

"Fiore?"

"Yes."

"Used to be a prosecutor in Norfolk County," Quirk said.

"She's with Cone Oakes now," I said.

"Good-looking broad," Quirk said.

"Yes."

"Good ass."

"You noticed."

"I'm a seasoned investigator," Quirk said. "Isn't she the one that's hot for you?"

"I hope so," I said.

CHAPTER THREE

We were walking toward the Cone Oakes conference room on the thirty-fifth floor. Today Rita had on a red jacket with a short leather skirt.

"You still with that prissy Jewess?" Rita said.

"I prefer to think of her as the girl of my dreams," I said.

"Even with me currently available?" Rita said.

"Again?"

"The bank guy didn't work out," Rita said. "Why not give it a whirl?"

"I'm emotionally limited," I said.

"Probably not," Rita said.

She opened the conference room door and we went in. Mary Smith was there with a young man.

The young man had on blue-tinted rimless glasses. He was nearly bald, and what hair remained he wore cut very short. He had a carefully trimmed blond mustache. He wore a dark gray pin-striped suit and a pale gray tie with a lavender shirt and a lavender pocket handkerchief. On the desk in front of him was a pigskin briefcase with a shoulder strap.

Mary was something else. Dark skin, big dark eyes, big blond hair, a lot of blue eye makeup. She had a big chest. She was in black as befit her recent widowhood. Her clothes were expensive but a little small for her. And the jacket of her black suit rode up a little on her hips. Rita introduced us. The guy was named Larson Graff.

"Mr. Graff is Mrs. Smith's public relations consultant," Rita said with a blank face.

I blinked once at her. Rita almost smiled but didn't.

"He's like family," Mary said. "You can say whatever you want."

Graff took a small tape recorder from his briefcase.

"You don't mind if we tape this, do you?" he said.

"I wish I'd known," I said. "I'd have brought my arrangements."

"What arrangements?" Mary said.

Graff said, "It's a joke, Mary."

Rita said, "I mind."

"Excuse me?" Graff said.

"I mind. This is privileged communication here. I don't want it taped."

"I thought it would be good to have a record," Graff said.

"It would not be good," Rita said.

Mary looked at Graff.

"Is there a problem?" she said.

"No. It's okay, Mary. Rita's just being careful."

"Well," Mary said. "Like I said, there's no need to be careful with Larson. He's family."

"Sure," I said. "Tell me about your husband's death, Mrs. Smith."

"Do I I have to?"

"No," I said.

"But you want me to?"

"Yes."

Graff put his hand on Mary's arm. "Mary," he said, "these people are trying to help you."

"I know they are, Larson. It's just, the whole subject is just so really, so really, really . . . icky."

I was quiet. Rita was quiet. Beyond the big glass windows of the conference room, the tops of the city were quiet. Off to the right I could see the river flowing past Cambridge.

"He died at home," I said.

"Yes. Louisburg Square. Nathan bought it when we got married. It's tripled, at least, in value."

"Real estate is always a sound investment," I said. "And you were in the house when he died."

"Yes. He was upstairs in the bedroom. I was in the library downstairs watching 'Survivor.' Do you watch that?"

"You bet," I said. "Was your door open?"

"Open?"

"Yes. The library door, was it open or closed?"

"I always close it. Nathan liked to sleep with his door open and the sound of the TV bothered him."

"And his bedroom is on the second floor?"

"The third. Nathan liked to get away from city sounds at night."

"Where did you sleep?"

She smiled a little and lowered her eyes.

"Why, aren't you nosy?" she said.

"I certainly am," I said.

"My bedroom was right next to Nathan's. We were very close. Just because we had separate rooms. We had a very full sex life."

"Everyone should," I said. "Tell me about when you found his body."

"Oh, don't say it that way. 'His body.' It sounds so, it's so really . . ."

I waited. Rita had rocked back in her chair, one spectacular leg crossed over the other. There was no expression on her face.

"How did you come across your, ah, late husband?" I said.

"I went up after the eleven-o'clock news," she said. "I always watch Channel Five when I'm home. I really like them. You watch Channel Five?"

"Day and night," I said. "You went up after the news?"

"Yes. I always do, and I always peek in, see if he's awake, so, if he is, I can say nighty-night to him."

"And you saw right away that he was deceased?"

"His light was on," she said.

She was the center of our attention. Her face had a kind of sweet dreaminess about it, as if reciting her story pleased her.

"Which is very unusual. Nathan usually goes to sleep very early. So I went in and, my God, there was blood everywhere on his pillow."

Her hands were resting on the tabletop in front of her. Graff patted one of them.

"It must have been so awful," he said.

"It was awful," Mary said.

We all sat for a time contemplating how awful it was.

"What did you do after you made this discovery?" I said.

"I don't . . . I guess I don't really remember. I think I burst into tears."

"Did you call the police?"

"Yes."

"How long after?"

"I don't know. Soon, I think."

"And no one else was in the house?"

"No."

"No one could have slipped in unnoticed?"

"Oh, I don't think so."

"Alarm system?"

"Yes. I guess. I don't know really. Nathan took care of that. I'm not very good about mechanical things."

I looked at Rita.

"Cops say the alarm was on," Rita said.

"Anyone have a key?" I said. "Or knowledge of the alarm code?"

"Alarm code?"

"The code you punch in to override the alarm," I said.

"I don't know what that means."

I nodded. "How about a key?" I said. "Who might have a key?"

"I have one."

"Good. Anyone else?"

"Nathan."

"Anyone else?"

"No. Nathan was very security-conscious. He didn't even give a key to Esther."

"Esther?"

Mary Smith nodded eagerly.

"Who's Esther?" I said.

"Our cleaning woman. I love her. She's so good."

"What if she came to clean and no one was there?"

"I don't know. I guess she'd have to come back."

"So just you and Nathan had a key to the house." I found myself speaking very slowly.

"Yes."

"And only Nathan knew the alarm code."

"I really just don't know how those things work," she said.

"So who shot him?" I said.

"I don't know."

She closed her eyes and sat perfectly still for a moment. "I don't even like to think about it," she said.

"I don't blame you," I said. "But we sort of have to think about it. Because the cops think you did it."

"I don't know how they can think that," she said.

I knew the remark was rhetorical. I let it pass. "You and Nathan get along well?" I said.

"Oh, yes. We were happy as clams."

"Cops say you tried to have him killed a while ago."

"I never did," she said. "I never did any such thing."

"You have a big fight with him the evening he was killed?"

"No."

"Cops have witnesses," I said.

"I don't care what they got, Nathan and I were happy as clams."

"Nathan have enemies?"

"No. Not at all. Everybody liked Nathan."

"Almost everybody," I said. "Anyone else in your life?"

"What do you mean by that?"

"Boyfriends?"

"No. Of course not. Absolutely not."

"How long you been married?" I said.

"Seven years."

"You going with anyone before you married him?"

"I dated, of course, I mean, look at me. Of course I dated."

"Anyone special?"

Her face brightened suddenly, and she smiled.

"They were all special," she said.

"See any of them since your marriage?"

"Well, of course, you don't give up all your friends when you get married."

"Maybe you could give us a list of your friends."

"My friends?"

"Somebody killed your husband."

"I can't give you a list of my friends. So you can go bother them?"

"I'm not your problem," I said. "I'm working for you. Won't your friends want to help you?"

"Well, of course."

I spread my hands. It follows as the night the day. She frowned for a while. Which was apparently what she did when she thought.

"Maybe I could give you a list," she said.

I waited. Finally she turned to her PR guy.

"Larson," she said. "You could give them the guest list for the last party."

"I have it in the computer," Graff said. "If that would help."

"Great," I said. "That'll be great."

I could see Rita off to the right. She looked amused.

CHAPTER FOUR

I went with Belson to the new Suffolk County House of Correction in South Bay, where they were holding Jack DeRosa for trial on an armed robbery charge.

"So, as I understand it," Belson said, "I'm trying to help you prove that our case against Mary Smith is no good."

"Yep."

"And what's in that for me?" Belson said. "I helped put the damned case together."

"Justice is served?"

"Yeah?"

"And I'm your pal."

"Oh boy," Belson said.

We met DeRosa in a secure conference room on the first floor.

His lawyer was with him. DeRosa was a small guy with a big nose that had been broken more than once. There was enough scar tissue around his eyes to suggest that he'd been a fighter.

"Welterweight?" I said.

"Yeah."

"Any good?" I said.

"I was a palooka," he said.

"So you found another line of work."

DeRosa shrugged. His jail fatigues were too big, and it made him look smaller than he was.

"Whaddya want?" he said.

"Woman named Mary Smith asked you to kill her husband," I said.

"Where'd you hear that?"

"From me," Belson said.

"We already have our deal in place," DeRosa's lawyer said.

She was stunning. Expensive blond hair cut short, dark blue pantsuit with a fine chalk line, white blouse, small diamond on a gold chain showing at her throat. She looked like she worked out, probably in bright tights and expensive sneakers.

"Where are you from?" I said to the lawyer.

"Excuse me?"

"What firm do you represent?"

"Kiley and Harbaugh," she said. "I'm Ann Kiley."

"Bobby Kiley's daughter?" I said.

"Yes."

"Wow!" I said.

"What can we do for you, Mr. Spenser?"

"I'm interested in who hooked DeRosa up with Mary Smith," I said.

"And what is your interest, Sergeant?"

"I'm just along to learn," Belson said.

"Are you here officially?"

"You mean if your client helps us out can I help him out?"

"Precisely."

"Sure."

She nodded slightly at DeRosa.

"Guy I know called me," DeRosa said. "Told me this broad was interested in a shooter."

"What's the guy's name?"

"Chuck."

"Chuck."

"Yeah. I don't know his last name, just Chuck."

"Where's Chuck from?"

"In town somewhere," DeRosa said.

"In town."

"Yeah."

"If I wanted to talk with Chuck, how would I reach him?"

"I don't know. He called me."

"So how'd you get in touch with Mary Smith?"

"Chuck give me her number," DeRosa said. "I called it."

I looked at Belson. He shrugged slightly.

"So," I said. "A guy named Chuck, you don't know his full name or how to reach him, calls you up and tells you that a woman

wants her husband killed, and you call her up and offer your services?"

"Yeah."

I looked at Belson again. He had no expression. I looked at Ann
Kiley. She seemed calm.

"Okay. Tell me about your conversation with Mary Smith."

"Hey, I already told about a hundred fucking cops and ADAs," he
said. "Didn't you read the reports?"

"It's just an excuse," I said. "You're so goddamned charming that
I just like to talk with you."

"Yeah, well, I don't like saying the same shit over and over."

"Sure," I said. "Like you got important stuff to do in here."

"It won't hurt," Ann Kiley said, "if you tell it once more, Jack."

"Yeah? Well, she met me at some fucking restaurant in a fucking
clothing store, for crissake."

"Okay. How'd you recognize her?"

"I asked the hostess, or whatever, and they seated me."

"What'd she say?"

"She just said she wanted her husband killed and could I do it?"

"How much she paying?"

"Fifty grand."

"Why didn't you take the job?"

"I did."

"But you didn't kill her husband."

"No."

"Because?"

"Because I don't do that kind of work."

"But you took the money."

"Yeah, sure. I figure I take the dough and don't do it. What's she gonna do?"

"And you have fifty large in your pocket," I said.

"Twenty-five. She give me half up front, half when it was done."

"She say why she wanted him killed?" I said.

"Nope."

"She ever follow up with you?" I said.

"No."

"So she gave you twenty-five thousand, and you put it in your pocket and walked away and never saw her again."

"That's right."

"How'd she give you the money?"

"Whaddya mean how? She fucking handed it to me."

"Cash?"

"Yeah. In a bag."

"Big bills?"

"Hundreds."

I went over it with him another time, and Belson tried him once. The story didn't change.

Finally Ann Kiley said, "I think it is clear that my client has told his story and he retells it consistently."

"I think you're right," I said.

"You'll speak to the district attorney," Ann Kiley said, "about my client's willingness to cooperate."

"Sure," Belson said.

As we walked to my car, I said to Belson, "Anything bother you?"

"Like what?" he said.

"Like an entry-level sluggo being represented by Kiley and Har-baugh," I said.

"Pro bono?" Belson said.

"You think?" I said.

"No."

"It bother you?"

"Sure it bothers me," Belson said. "And it bothers me that he got into the deal through a guy named Chuck whom we can't iden-tify, and it bothers me that his story is so exactly the same every time. And it bothers me his lawyer let him keep talking about it with only my sort of casual comment that I'd speak to the DA."

"I noticed that myself," I said.

"However," Belson said, "sergeants don't get to be lieutenants by helping people unsolve a high-profile murder."

"True," I said.

"But, I'm not forgetting what I owe you. . . . When Lisa was gone."

"That's not an owesie," I said.

"It is to me. I'll help you when I can."

"Mary Smith says she never hired this guy," I said.

"Mary Smith's an idiot," Belson said.

"Well," I said. "There's that."

CHAPTER FIVE

Larson Graff faxed me an invitation list with the names of Mary Smith's 227 closest friends, in alphabetical order. I recognized enough of the names to assume that these weren't people who hung out at bowling alleys.

The first one I was able to talk with was a guy named Loren Bannister, who was the CEO of an insurance company. He probably thought I was a prospect.

"Mary Smith?" he said.

"Yes, sir. Your name was high on her list."

"Maybe because the list was alphabetical," he said.

Bannister was square-jawed and silver-haired with a nice tan. He was in full uniform. Dark suit, white shirt, gold cuff links, red tie with tiny white dots.

"You're too modest," I said.

"Um-hm. I assume this is connected with Nathan Smith's death?"

"Yes."

"She really kill him?" Bannister said.

"No."

"And you work for Cone Oakes?"

"Yes."

"Barry Cone called me," Bannister said. "How can I help you?"

"Tell me about Mary Smith."

"Well, I don't know her very well," Bannister said. "I knew Nathan a little."

"They seem happy to you?"

"Sure. I guess so. She was younger. As I said, I'd see them now and then, at charity events, mostly."

"Did you know them socially?"

"In the sense that we would go out to dinner with them? No."

"Do you know Larson Graff?"

"Graff?"

"Yes."

"I don't believe so. Who is he?"

"He's Mary Smith's PR man."

Bannister smiled. "Oh," he said. "Him."

"You know him?"

"I didn't know his name," Bannister said. "Mary is at a lot of affairs without Nathan. Whatsisname escorts her."

"Did your company insure the Smiths?"

"I don't really know," Bannister said. He smiled. "I don't do much direct selling."

"Could you find out?" I said.

"Does it say CEO on my door?" he said. "Of course I could find out."

"Would you?"

Bannister looked as if he might say no. But instead he picked up his phone.

"Allison? Please find out if we have policies on Nathan Smith or Mary Smith." He looked at me. "Address?"

I gave him the address and he repeated it to Allison.

"Get back to me promptly," he said and hung up. He seemed confident that he would be gotten back to promptly.

"Aside from walker duties," I said, "would you know why Mary Smith would need a public relations person?"

"No."

"Who would know?" I said.

Bannister leaned back in his swivel chair and clasped his hands behind his head.

"Barry Cone's a buddy of mine," Bannister said. "He asked me to talk with you. I'm happy to do so. But I don't get why you're talking to me. I don't really know Mary Smith. I don't know who would know about her. I say hello to her at cocktail parties that I go to because being prominent is part of my job."

"And Nathan Smith?"

"See him at the Harvard Club once in a while," Bannister said. "Knew him casually. He was a player."

"A player?"

"Yes. In the money business."

"What did he do?" I said.

Bannister smiled. "He fiddled with money."

"How?"

"Like everybody else," Bannister said. "He bought and he sold."

"Stocks and bonds?"

"And real estate, and banks, and, for all I know, lottery tickets."

"Who would know more about him?" I said.

Bannister shrugged. "His attorney. His broker. His doctor. His priest? I don't know how to make this clearer. I don't really know either one of them."

The phone rang and Bannister answered. He listened, made a couple of notes, said thank you, and hung up.

"We have a whole-life policy on Nathan Smith," he said.

"How much?"

Bannister hesitated only a moment. "Ten million dollars," he said.

"There's some premiums to pay," I said.

"Not as much as you might think," Bannister said. "It was taken out for him at birth, by his grandfather."

"Beneficiary?"

"Mary Smith."

I didn't say anything. Bannister had tilted back in his chair again and reclasped his hands.

"That doesn't help your cause," Bannister said.

"Not much," I said. "Can I get a copy of the policy?"

"It's confidential."

"Yeah, but you and Barry Cone are buddies."

Bannister smiled. "I'll have somebody run it off and FedEx it over," he said. "May I ask a question?"

"Sure."

"Why, if you are trying to clear Mary Smith, are you investigating Mary Smith?"

"I have nowhere else to investigate," I said. "Think of it as cold-canvassing."

Bannister smiled. "I never sold insurance," he said. "My last job was at Pepsi-Cola."

"Management is management," I said.

Bannister nodded and smiled. "Good luck with the cold canvass," he said.

CHAPTER SIX

It was almost May. The azaleas were blooming. The swan boats were active in the Public Gardens. The softball leagues had begun across Charles Street, on the Common. And, in the Charles River Basin, the little rental sailboats skidded and heeled in the faint evening wind.

"You're working for that hussy again," Susan said.

"Rita?"

"Miss Predatory," Susan said.

"I like Rita," I said.

"I know."

"Are you being jealous?" I said.

"Analytic," Susan said. "Rita is sexually rapacious and perfectly amoral about it. I'm merely acknowledging that."

"But you don't disapprove."

"Professionalism prevents disapproval," Susan said.

"So the term 'hussy' is just a clinical designation," I said.

"Certainly," Susan said. "She has every right to wear her skirts as short as she wishes."

"She wears short skirts?" I said.

"Like you didn't notice."

"So do you like Rita, Ms. Professional?"

"Red-haired floozy," Susan said.

"I so admire professionalism."

Susan and I stood on the little barrel-arched bridge over the lagoon and watched Pearl the Wonder Dog as she tracked the elusive french-fry carton. Her face was gray. She didn't hear well. Her back end was arthritic and she limped noticeably as she hunted.

"Old," Susan said to me.

I nodded.

"But her eyes are still bright and she still wags her tail and gives kisses," Susan said.

"Me too."

"I've been meaning to speak to you about the tail wagging," Susan said.

Pearl found a nearly bald tennis ball under the island end of the bridge and picked it up and brought it to us and refused to drop it. So we patted her and Susan told her she was very good, until Pearl spotted a pigeon, lost interest in the ball, dropped it, and limped after the pigeon.

"She hasn't got long," Susan said.

"No."

"Then what do we do?"

"If she has to be put away, can you do it?" I said.

"Yes."

"Good."

"Because you can't?"

"I don't know about can't," I said. "But if you can do it, I'll let you."

"I thought you were fearless," Susan said.

"I am, but it's embarrassing for a guy as fearless as I am to cry in the vet's office."

"But it's okay for me?"

"Sure," I said. "You're a girl."

"How enlightened," Susan said.

Pearl came back to check where we were. Since her hearing had declined she was more careful about checking on us. Susan bent over and looked at her face.

"But not yet," Susan said.

"No."

Susan put her arms around my waist and pressed her face against my chest. I patted her back softly. After a while she pushed away from me and looked up. Her face was bright. The shadow had moved on.

"Okay," she said.

"Okay."

"I'm hungry," she said.

"I have cold chicken and fruit salad," I said. "And I could make some biscuits."

We had to wait until Pearl looked at us and then gesture her to come. When she arrived Susan snapped her leash back on and we headed slowly, which was Pearl's only pace, back toward Marlborough Street.

"Do you really think Mary Smith didn't do it?" Susan said.

"I'm sort of required to," I said. "Ah, professionally."

Susan gave me a look. "But when you're not being professional," Susan said. "Like now."

"I wish there was another explanation for how Nathan Smith got shot to death in a locked house with his wife downstairs, and she didn't hear a thing."

"So why do you think she didn't do it? Other than professionalism."

"It just doesn't feel right. She doesn't feel right. If she did it, wouldn't she have a better alibi than *I was downstairs watching Channel Five?*"

"You said she wasn't very bright."

"She appears to be very dumb," I said. "But wouldn't she have at least faked a break-in? Window broken? Door lock jimmied? Something? How dumb is dumb?"

Susan smiled. "I would say that there is no bottom to dumb."

"You shrinks are so judgmental," I said.

"Maybe," she said. "But some of us are sexually accomplished."

"Nice talk," I said. "In front of Pearl."

"Pearl's deaf as a turnip," Susan said.

"And a blessing it is," I said.

CHAPTER SEVEN

I went back to my list of names. A number of Mary Smith's 226 other best friends didn't know her at all. They could be handled by phone. Some weren't available. Some needed to be called on. None appeared to be an ex-boyfriend. The last call I made was to a woman named Clarice Taggert, who was the director of corporate giving at Illinois Federal Bank. I met her in the bank cafeteria, where she was drinking coffee at a table near the door. I had described myself on the phone and she stood when I came in.

"You said you looked like Cary Grant," she said.

"You recognized me when I came in," I said.

She grinned. "You don't look like a banker," she said. "Want coffee?"

We took our coffee to a table. She was a strong-looking black woman in a pale gray pantsuit with a white blouse. She wore a gold chain around her neck. There was a wide gold wedding band on the appropriate finger.

"What can I do for you?" she said.

"Tell me about Mary Smith, Ms. Taggert."

"Clarice," she said. "You don't vamp around much, do you?"

"I did that on the phone," I said.

"Mary Smith was a very good hit for various charities."

"She was generous?"

"More than that," Clarice said. "She was generous with her own money, and active in getting other people to give."

"How so?"

"She was always eager to throw a fund-raising party."

"Like?"

"One of the things she did was to host a gourmet dinner at her elegant home in Louisburg Square, prepared by a celebrity chef from one of the restaurants. Sometimes there would be a celebrity there—sports, local television, politics, whoever they could snare. And people would pay X amount of dollars to attend. They'd get a fancy meal, and a house tour, and, if there was a celebrity, the chance to eat dinner with him or her."

"That's why she has a PR guy," I said.

"You have to understand Mary," Clarice said. "She isn't very bright."

"That I understand," I said.

"And she has no training in being a rich upper-class lady."

"Which she wasn't," I said, "until she married Nathan Smith."

"Exactly."

"And the charity work?" I said.

"Part of becoming a wealthy Boston lady."

I nodded. Clarice drank some coffee. Her eyes were big and dark. She had on a nice perfume.

"Where'd she grow up?" I said.

"I think someone told me she lived in Franklin."

"I asked her for a list of her friends," I said. "She gave me a guest list, on which you are the final name. You a friend of hers?"

"Not really. Each year, the bank designates a certain sum of money to be distributed to deserving charities. I'm the one decides who gets it."

"So she woos you for your money."

"The bank's money," Clarice said. "But yes."

"You wouldn't put her on a list of your best friends."

"I don't dislike her. I feel kind of sorry for her."

"Because?"

"Because she's entirely confused by the world as it is. She thinks it is like the one she has seen in the movies and the women's magazines. She's always been sexy, and she thinks it matters in the world she's entered."

"Gee," I said. "It does in my world."

"I would guess that," she said. "But not in the world of the wealthy Boston lady."

"What matters there?"

"Money, pedigree, or the illusion of pedigree."

"How do you fare in that world," I said.

"I don't aspire to it," she said.

I nodded again. The room was full of well-dressed women getting coffee and salads. Most of them were young and in shape. Young professional women were a good-looking lot.

"Cute, aren't they," Clarice said.

I grinned. "So, would you put Mary Smith on a list of friends?"

She smiled. "I guess I wouldn't."

We were both quiet, drinking our coffee.

"Do you think she has friends?" I said.

"I think she thinks the people on her guest list are friends," Clarice said.

"And the people she knew in Franklin?"

"Low-class would be my guess," Clarice said.

My coffee cup was empty. So was Clarice's. I remained alert to the panorama of young professional women.

"Sex apparently does matter in your world," Clarice said.

"Does to me," I said.

"Are you married?"

"Sort of."

"How can you be 'sort of' married?" Clarice said.

"We're not married, but we're monogamous."

"Except for the roving eye," Clarice said.

"Except for that," I said.

"Live together?"

"Not quite."

"Love each other?"

"Yes."

"How long you been together?" Clarice said.

"About twenty-five years."

"So why don't you get married?"

"Damned if I know," I said.

CHAPTER EIGHT

Pequod Savings and Loan was essentially a suburban bank. It had branches in Concord, Lexington, Lynnfield, and Weston. There was a home branch next to a gourmet takeout shop on the first floor of a good-looking recycled manufacturing building in East Cambridge, near Kendall Square. A clerk passed me on to a bank officer who questioned me closely and passed me on to the home-office manager. In less than an hour I was sitting in the office of the vice president for public affairs.

She was a good-looking smallish woman with thick auburn hair and large dark eyes and a wide mouth. She was wearing a pale beige suit. Her nails gleamed with polish. She had a big diamond on her right hand. An engraved brass sign on her desk read AMY PETERS.

"Would you care for coffee?" she said.

I had decided to cut back on coffee. Three cups in the morning was plenty.

"Yes," I said. "Cream and sugar."

"How about milk and sugar?" she said.

"Oh well."

She stood and went out of the office. The pants of her beige suit were well-fitted. On her desk was a picture of two small children. On a shelf in the bookcase behind her desk was a picture of her with Bobby Orr. There was also a plaque recognizing her as *Pequod Person of the Year*. When she came back in carrying the coffee, she brought with her the vague scent of good cologne. She gave me one cup and took the other around behind her desk and sat and had a sip.

"So," she said. "You are a private detective."

I had some coffee. It wasn't very good. I had some more.

"I am," I said.

She smiled. Her teeth were even and very white.

"And what are you detecting here at the bank?" she said.

"You know that Nathan Smith has died," I said.

"Yes. I understand that he was murdered."

"Do you understand by whom?" I said.

"Whom? What kind of private detective says 'whom'?"

"Handsome intrepid ones," I said.

She looked at me steadily for a moment, as if deciding whether to buy me. Then she smiled a little. "The papers say it was his wife."

"They do," I said.

"And what do you say?"

"I say I don't know. Tell me about Nathan Smith."

"Whom do you represent?" she said and smiled, pleased with herself for saying "whom."

"I'm employed by Mary Smith's attorney," I said.

"So you are predisposed to assume she's innocent."

"Me and the legal system," I said.

"Oh . . . yes . . . of course."

"So what was Nathan Smith like?" I said.

"He owned this bank," she said. "His father owned it before him and I don't know how many generations back beyond that."

"Un-huh. So who owns it now?"

"His estate, I assume."

"Who's running it now?"

"Our CEO," she said, "Marvin Conroy."

"Does he have any ownership?" I said.

She nodded. "He's a minority stockholder," she said.

"How about you?"

She smiled. "I'm an employee."

"Any other minority stockholders?"

"Frankly, I don't know. I'm here for public relations. I'm not privy to all of the arrangements Mr. Smith made."

"It sounds like there were some," I said.

"If there were I don't know of them," Amy Peters said.

"But you might speculate?"

"Public relations directors don't get ahead if they make improprietous speculations."

"What kind of banker says 'improprietous'?" I said.

She smiled and there was in the smile the same sense I'd had before, that she was considering whether I'd be worth the purchase price.

"Handsome sexy ones," she said.

"I'm a detective," I said. "I already noticed the handsome part."

"And the sexy part?"

"I surmised that."

"Good," she said.

I smiled my most engaging smile at her. If you have an ace you may as well play it. Oddly, Amy Peters remained calm.

"What sort of private arrangements could a banker make?" I said.

"I'm sure I don't know."

"Have you been with the bank long?" I said.

"Ten years."

"Before that?"

"I did PR for Sloan, Simpson."

"Brokerage house?" I said.

"Yes. Am I a suspect?"

I smiled. Just the routine smile. If the A smile hadn't overwhelmed her, I saw no reason to waste it.

"No."

"Then why ask?"

"Information is the capital of my work," I said. "I don't know what will matter."

She nodded.

"I went to Middlebury College, and Harvard Business School. I have two daughters. I'm divorced."

"So you knew Nathan Smith before he was married."

"I knew him professionally. He didn't spend a lot of time at the bank, and when he was here, he didn't spend a lot of time with the help."

"Who did he spend time with?"

"I don't really know. I work here. I worked for him. My job is to present the bank to the public in as favorable an image as I can. I do not keep track of the owner, for God's sake."

"And you're doing a hell of a job of it," I said.

She started to speak and stopped. "Goddamn you," she said.

"Me?"

"You. I am supposed to be a professional and you've waltzed in here and smiled a big smile and showed me your muscles and all my professionalism seems to have fluttered right out the window."

"I didn't show you my muscles," I said.

"I saw them anyway," she said. Beneath her perfect makeup there seemed to be a hint of color along her cheekbones.

"Are you married?" she said.

"I'm, ah, going steady," I said.

"Going steady? I haven't heard anyone say that in thirty years."

I shrugged.

"How long have you been *going steady*?"

" 'Bout twenty-five years," I said. "With a little time out in the middle."

She leaned back a little in her chair and looked at me in silence for a considerable time.

Finally she said, "Of all the banks, in all the world, you had to walk into this one."

"We'll always have Cambridge," I said.

CHAPTER NINE

There had been something lurking behind what Amy Peters had said. She knew something about Nathan Smith. I didn't know what it was yet. I drove out of the parking garage next to the bank. A moment of brightness flicked past me from across the street and I looked over at a black Volvo sedan across from the entrance. I thought I saw binoculars, which would account for the reflected flash. I turned onto Broadway toward the Longfellow Bridge. The car didn't move. As I got on the bridge I checked the rearview mirror and the Volvo was there, two cars back.

I punched up the number for the Harbor Health Club on the car phone. Henry Cimoli answered.

"Hawk there?" I said.

"Yeah," Henry said. "Intimidating the patrons."

"What's he doing?" I said.

"Nothing."

"Let me talk to him," I said.

In a moment Hawk said, "Un-huh?" into his end of the phone.

"I'm on the Longfellow Bridge," I said. "I think I'm being tailed by a black Volvo. Mass plates, number 73622. I'm going to park at the health club and go in. I want you to pick up the Volvo, if they leave. See who they are."

"You care if they see me?" Hawk said.

"Yes."

"Okay," Hawk said.

On the Boston end of the bridge, to make sure, I went straight up Cambridge Street and through Bowdoin Square and down New Sudbury Street and back down Canal Street toward the Fleet. On Causeway Street I turned right and headed back through the North End. It was a way to get to the Harbor Health Club that no one would take. The black Volvo was still behind me.

When I started at the Harbor Health Club I was still boxing, and it was a dark ugly gym where fighters trained. Now I wasn't boxing anymore. The club was three stories high, and they had valet parking. I gave my car to the valet and headed in. I didn't see Hawk. But I didn't expect to. Inside I went up to the second floor where there was a women-only weight room across from the snack bar and cocktail lounge, and looked down into the street from the front windows. The Volvo was there, idling across the street.

Henry, wearing a white T-shirt and white satin sweatpants, joined me at the window. Henry used to box lightweight, and it showed in the scar tissue around his eyes and the way his nose had thickened. The T-shirt showed how muscular he still was. Which is not a bad thing in a health-club owner.

"Hawk already left," Henry said.

"I know."

"You working on something?"

"I am."

Henry looked down through the window. "The black Volvo tailing you?"

"Un-huh."

"What kinda crook tails somebody in a Volvo?" Henry said.

"Hawk's going to tell us," I said.

"I get it," Henry said. "You ditch them here and Hawk picks them up and then you've got a tail on the tail."

"Pretty smart," I said. "For a guy who got whacked in the face as much as you did."

"Never got knocked down though," Henry said. "You gonna work out?"

"Maybe later," I said. "Isn't it sexist to have a women-only weight room?"

"I think so," Henry said.

The Volvo waited for two and a half hours, into the rush hour, until a cop pulled his cruiser up behind it and gave a short wail on his siren and gestured them to move the car. Which they did.

I looked down at the evening commuter traffic trying to jam past the Big Dig construction for a while and then went to the snack bar and had a turkey burger. Healthful.

I called Frank Belson while I waited and asked him to check the plate numbers on the Volvo. I ate another turkey burger. Belson called me back. After two hours and twenty minutes, Hawk came into the snack bar and slid onto the stool beside me.

"Went down to Braintree," Hawk said. "Shopping center right there where 3 and 128 fork off the expressway. Parked in the lot. Got out, got in another car, drove back up the expressway to a place called Soldiers Field Development Limited."

"Would that be on Soldiers Field Road?" I said.

"How'd you guess that?" Hawk said.

I smiled modestly and looked at the floor.

"You get the plate number?" I said.

"You didn't tell me to get no license plate number," Hawk said.

"I was being racially sensitive," I said. "I didn't want to sound patronizing."

"Yassah," Hawk said and recited the plate number. Hawk never wrote anything down. As far as I could tell he never forgot anything.

"You get anything on the car they dumped?" Hawk said.

"Stolen car," I said.

"They being careful," Hawk said. "Tail you with stolen car. Dump it. Swap cars."

"Not careful enough," I said.

" 'Course not," Hawk said. "How they gonna be careful enough when they up against you and me?"

"They didn't make you?" I said.

Hawk looked at me without speaking.

"No," I said. "Of course they didn't. They actually go in the development company?"

"Un-huh."

"And didn't go right on through and come out the front and get in a waiting car and drive off?" I said. "Leaving you confused and uncertain?"

"Un-un."

"You got a good look at them?"

"Un-huh."

"So you'd recognize them if you saw them again."

It wasn't a question, I was just thinking out loud. Hawk made no response.

"Okay so we know who," I said. "Be good to find out why."

"It would," Hawk said. "Maybe next time they follow you we can stop and ask them."

"We'll see," I said.

CHAPTER TEN

I was in my office tilted back in my chair with my feet up drinking a cup of coffee and eating my second corn muffin while I reread the list of Mary Smith's closest friends. The sunlight sprawled its familiar light across my desk. Behind me I had the window open and the pleasant traffic sounds drifted up from the point where Berkeley Street intersects with Boylston. There was nothing new. Still no names with asterisks indicating a possible murderer. Just a bunch of mostly Anglo-Saxon names with mostly business addresses. One of the business addresses was Soldiers Field Development Ltd. *Oh ho!* I had taken to saying *Oh ho!* in moments like this ever since Susan had suggested that *ah ha!* was corny. The address was for someone named Felton Shawcross, who was listed as CEO. I took a bite of corn muffin. It's hard to think when you're hungry. It is also hard to think when you don't have anything to think about. Something might develop out of the clue. But right now it was just a clue.

I finished my corn muffin, drank the last of my coffee, washed my hands and face, and headed off down Berkeley Street toward the South End. By the time I crossed Columbus Ave. I knew I was being followed again, on foot this time. A dark curly-haired guy with a big mustache had gotten out of a black Chrysler sedan as soon as I had come out of my building. The sedan had been double-parked in front of FAO Schwarz on the corner of Boylston and Berkeley, and pulled away down Boylston right after Curly got out. He was so conscientious in paying me no attention that I spotted him almost at once. Though in his defense, I suppose, I was looking for him. Berkeley Street was one way the other way, so I knew that if they were tailing me again, it would have to be on foot. Larson Graff's place of business was a red brick row house on Appleton Street. The office was on the first floor. Graff lived above the store. Graff's desk was in the bow window of a room that was probably once the dining room. It was a vast pale oak piece, with thickly turned legs. The window behind it was punctuated occasionally with panes of stained glass. Through it I could see Curly standing innocently across the street talking on his cell phone.

Graff was immaculate in a double-breasted blue blazer, a yellow silk tie, and a starched white broadcloth shirt. He stood to shake my hand.

"Mr. Spenser," he said. "How nice to see you again."

"Everybody says that."

Graff smiled uncertainly. "Well," he said. "I'm sure they mean it."

He gestured me toward a client chair. I sat. Maybe it was better not to kid with Larson.

"I wanted to thank you for the list of names you sent over on behalf of Mary Smith," I said.

"Oh, no problem. Just run it off on the computer, you know."

"Yes. Do you know anybody that's friendly with Mrs. Smith who is not on the list?"

Graff's eyes widened.

"Not on the list?"

"Yeah. Maybe a pal from the old neighborhood? People she used to play miniature golf with?"

"Miniature golf?"

"Maybe an old boyfriend?"

"Perhaps you should ask Mrs. Smith."

"Oh, I will," I said. "This is just background. Make sure to touch all bases and all that."

Graff nodded as if he weren't so sure.

"You must know a name," I said. "One name."

It's an old trick, ask for one name, implying that if you get it you'll go away and leave them alone. Graff fell for it.

"Well, there's Roy," he said.

"And there's Siegfried," I said.

Graff looked as if he didn't find me amusing. It was a look I've grown familiar with.

"Roy Levesque," Graff said. "I believe she went to high school with him."

"Do you have an address for Roy?" I said.

"I believe he lives in Franklin."

Through the window I could see the Chrysler sedan cruise up and pause in front of where Curly was standing.

"Anybody else?" I said.

"You said one name."

"I'm not very trustworthy," I said. "You must know one more name."

He didn't bite the second time. Most of the time they don't. But the effort was there.

"I'm dreadfully sorry, Mr. Spenser, I really don't. I'm sure Mrs. Smith can help you."

"I'm sure," I said. "When you accompany her socially, are you paid for your time?"

Graff looked like he wanted to hang one on my kisser, though it seemed unlikely that he would.

"I am on retainer to Mrs. Smith," Graff said.

"To do what?" I said.

"She has a very crowded and committed social calendar," Graff said. "I help her organize it."

Graff sounded as if he were not as pleased to see me as he had said he was when I came in.

"How about Mr. Smith?"

"He was not as socially oriented as Mrs. Smith."

Outside the Chrysler moved away from Curly and cruised slowly down Appleton toward Berkeley. Curly remained, strolling up and down looking at roof lines, admiring the architecture.

"You and Mr. Smith friendly?" I said.

Graff looked offended. "Why do you ask?"

"I have no idea," I said. "I'm just a gabby guy."

"Oh, I'm sure," Graff said.

"So were you friendly?"

"He was always a gentleman," Graff said.

"But?"

"But nothing at all. I worked for Mrs. Smith. Mr. Smith was always pleasant. I don't know him very well."

"How about Marvin Conroy?"

"I'm sorry, I don't know him."

"Amy Peters?"

Graff shook his head. "I'm sorry, Mr. Spenser, but I really must cut this short. I have a client meeting that I'm already late for."

"With whom?" I said.

"That is really none of your business, Mr. Spenser."

I fought back the impulse to say, *Well, I'm making it my business.* Susan would be proud of me. I stood. We shook hands. And I went out to take Curly for a walk.

CHAPTER

ELEVEN

Once you know you're being tailed it is easy to spot it. Today we were cruising along Route 495. Me and my shadow. They were driving another black car, an Explorer. Everybody uses black cars for surveillance. Like somehow a black car wouldn't be noticed. Maybe it's the movies. At Route 140 we turned off toward Franklin. According to the phone book Roy Levesque still lived there.

The address was a green shingled ranch near the college. A narrow concrete walk led up to the house. The lawn was neat, and a big hydrangea with blue flowers bloomed beside the front door. I parked out front. The black Explorer drove on past, with Curly in the passenger seat, carefully looking the other way.

I went up the concrete walk and stood on the low concrete front step and rang the doorbell. A burly woman with gray hair opened the door. She was wearing a flowered dress that reached her ankles.

"Hi," I said brightly, "I'm looking for Roy Levesque."

She had a pale indoor face and thick black eyebrows that almost met over the bridge of her broad nose.

"Why?"

"I'd like to talk with him about Mary Toricelli."

The woman looked like she had smelled a bad thing. Maybe it was Mary. Maybe she always looked that way.

"What about her?"

"Is Roy home?"

She thought about that for a moment.

"He's eatin' his breakfast," she said. "He works nights."

"Maybe I could join him for coffee," I said.

That seemed too hard a thing for her to think about. She tried for a while and gave up and yelled into the house. "Roy. Some guy here wants to see you."

Roy appeared in an undershirt and baggy jeans with no belt. His long hair was clubbed back in a ponytail. He was barefoot and needed a shave. On his upper arm was a tattoo of a cowboy riding a bucking horse. The cowboy was holding the reins with one hand and waving his hat with the other. Below the horse, a banner read "Born to Raise Hell."

"Whaddya need?" Roy said.

"I need to talk about Mary Toricelli."

He looked at me for a moment without speaking. You could tell he thought he was scary. Then he spoke to the woman.

"Ma," he said. "Whyn't you go clean up the breakfast dishes."

She shuffled off in her blue rubber flip-flops. Roy stepped out onto the front stoop and closed the door behind him.

"Go ahead," Roy said. "Talk."

"I understand you are a friend of Mary's."

"Who tole you that?"

"She did," I lied.

"And who the fuck are you," Roy said.

"My name is Spenser," I said. "I'm trying to clear her of a murder charge."

"Yeah, I heard about her husband. What are you coming to me for?"

"I understand you used to go out with her."

"Yeah?"

"Are you still friends?"

"I seen her once, couple years ago, at a high school reunion," Roy said.

He was dark-haired and taller than I was, with dark eyes that looked tired, and a little pouchy. I thought he looked like a boozer. Some women might think he looked soulful.

"Seen her since?" I said.

"None of your fucking business," Roy said.

"Clever answer," I said. "You go to high school together?"

"Yeah. Graduated Franklin High in 'eighty-nine," Levesque said. "You a fucking cop, man?"

"Private," I said.

"Private? A fucking gumshoe? For crissake I'm trying to eat my breakfast."

"The reunion the last time you saw her?"

"I don't know. I seen her when I seen her."

"You anything more than friends?"

"What's that mean?"

"You intimate?"

"You mean did I fuck her?"

"Yes."

"What if I did?"

"More power to you," I said.

"I didn't say I fucked her. I just said what if I did?"

"Sure," I said.

"I don't want to get mixed up in some freaking murder case, you know?"

"I know," I said. "She date anyone else besides you?"

"No . . . I don't know . . . I never said I dated her."

"But you did."

"I don't have to talk with you, pal."

"Of course you don't," I said. "You know anybody she might have been dating?"

"I got nothing else to say."

"What a shame," I said.

"So just shove fucking off, pal."

"You bet," I said. "How'd you feel about her marrying Nathan Smith?"

He tapped me on the chest with a long forefinger. "I told you once to take a walk. I'm not telling you again."

"Actually you told me to 'shove fucking off.' You didn't say anything about taking a walk."

Roy looked a little confused. But he was a tough guy, wasn't he? He changed the jabbing finger into a flat hand on my chest and shoved. I didn't move. There was no point to this. He wasn't going to talk to me anymore. I was just being stubborn.

Roy said, "You don't want to fuck with me, pal."

"Why not?"

"Because you're real close to a lot of trouble."

"You?" I said.

"Yeah. Me."

"Roy, you couldn't cause me trouble if you had a bulldozer."

Roy was maybe an inch taller than I was, but ten pounds lighter. He thought about it. But he didn't do it. Instead he said, "Ahh," and dismissed me with a hand gesture and turned back toward the house.

"We'll talk again," I said.

He kept going.

As I went back to my car I saw the nose of the Explorer around the corner on a side street. I thought about going over and grabbing one of the shadows. But that was just irritation. It wouldn't produce anything good.

Nothing else had.

CHAPTER

TWELVE

Susan had decided we should ride bikes. So we rented a couple, to see how we liked it, and set out.

"We'll just ride along the river a little ways," Susan had said. "And then we can sit and have our little lunch, and then ride back. It'll be fun."

"Did you know that bike riding is a threat to male fertility?" I said.

"That doesn't matter."

"How about a threat to potency?"

"That would matter," Susan said.

We rode past the Harvard Business School on the Boston side of the river, heading into town. The balance was still a little shaky, but I knew it would come. There wasn't room on the trail to ride beside each other. Bikes coming in the other direction couldn't get by. So I trailed along behind her, admiring her butt in its spandex tights. It was not fun. I hadn't ridden a bicycle since I was a kid in Wyoming, and after five minutes on this one I was glad I hadn't. We went over the Weeks footbridge to the Cambridge side again, and stopped and sat on benches near the Harvard women's boathouse. Susan took a brown paper bag out of her backpack and began to set out finger sandwiches.

"There," Susan said. "Was that fun?"

"What would be fun about it?" I said. "We're not even together while we're riding."

"You're just afraid you'll fall off and embarrass yourself."

"I thought you thought I was fearless," I said.

"About stuff that matters," she said. "But when it doesn't matter, you hate doing things at which you're not accomplished."

"Shall I lean back, Doc, and recall my childhood?"

Susan took a small bite of her egg salad sandwich. "I have all the information about you I require," she said. "Tell me about the Nathan Smith business you're working on."

"There's a lot wrong with the Nathan Smith business," I said. "First of all, there's someone following me."

"Dangerous?"

"No," I said. "It's a what's-he-up-to tail, rather than a try-to-kill-him tail."

"Oh good," Susan said. "Do they know you've spotted them?"

"I don't think so," I said. "They're still being covert. If they knew I'd made them they wouldn't bother."

"And you think it relates to the Nathan Smith murder?"

"Started shortly after I took the case," I said.

"Do you know who they are?"

"They're connected to a company called Soldiers Field Development Limited, the CEO of which is on Mary Smith's invitation list."

I took a second finger sandwich from the bag.

"What's here besides bread and ham?" I said.

"Butter."

"Butter?"

"Well, not exactly butter. I sprayed it with one of those no-calorie butter-flavored sprays. Same thing."

"Jesus," I said.

"Is it possible that it's a coincidence, the surveillance and stuff? Or maybe connected to another case you were involved in? A loose end somewhere?"

"Always possible," I said. "I leave enough loose ends. On the other hand, what do you shrinks think about coincidences?"

"They occur, but it is not a good idea to assume them."

"That's what we sleuths think about them, too," I said.

"So if this were the open-and-shut it seems to be," Susan said, "why would anyone follow you?"

"Why indeed?" I said.

"Do you have a theory?"

"Nothing so grand," I said. "The tail aside, there's a lot I don't like about this. I don't like how lousy Mary Smith's alibi is. I don't like the sense I get that there's a lot I'm not being told."

"By whom?"

"By Mary Smith. By a guy named Roy Levesque that she was in high school with. By a guy named DeRosa who says Mary asked him to kill Nathan. By the woman I talked with at Nathan's bank. Nice woman, Amy Peters."

"As nice as I am?" Susan said.

"Of course not," I said. "She has information, or at least a theory, that she's not sharing. So does Mary Smith's PR guy. I'd also like to figure out why a stiff like DeRosa is represented by an attorney from Kiley and Harbaugh."

"But you have a plan," Susan said.

"I always have a plan," I said.

"Let me guess," she said. "I'll bet you plan to keep blundering along annoying people, and see what happens."

"Wow," I said. "You shrinks can really read a guy."

"Magical, isn't it," she said.

CHAPTER THIRTEEN

I was on the low doorstep of a three-decker on Lithgow Street off Codman Square, looking for Esther Morales. She opened the door on my second ring, a small tan woman with bright intelligent eyes.

"Sí?"

"My name is Spenser," I said. "I'm working for Mary Smith. You do her housecleaning."

"I clean for Mr. Smith," she said. "Fifteen years."

"Not Mrs. Smith?"

"She come along. I clean for her, too."

"The police think she murdered her husband. What do you think?"

"I think I am very impolite. Please come into my house."

"Thank you."

She took me to the kitchen in the back of the house and made me some coffee. The woodwork and cabinets were stained a dark brown and gleamed with many coats of varnish. The vinyl tile flooring was made to look like quarry tile and gleamed with many coats of wax. I sat at a glistening white metal kitchen table and drank from a mug with a Red Sox logo on it.

Esther Morales sat across the table from me and had some coffee, too.

"Are you with the police?" she said.

"No," I said. "I'm a private detective hired by the lawyer who represents Mrs. Smith."

"So you are trying to help Mrs. Smith?"

"I'm sort of trying to find out the truth of what happened," I said.

"She killed him."

"You know that?"

"Yes."

"Tell me what you know," I said.

"Mr. Smith was a very nice man. He was very pleasant. He paid me well and gave me nice presents on the holidays."

I nodded.

"Then she came," Esther said.

"Yes?"

"She is not nice."

"How so?" I said.

Esther frowned. I realized that she didn't understand the expression.

"What wasn't nice about her?" I said.

"She was bossy. She yelled at me. She yelled at Mr. Smith."

"What did she yell about?"

"She would yell about money."

Why should they be different.

"Anything else?" I said.

"I could not always hear them and, sometimes, when people speak too fast or speak oddly, my English . . ." She shrugged.

"How about Mr. Smith? He ever yell at her?" I said.

"No. He was very kind to her. Sometimes she would make him cry."

"They have friends over?"

"She did," Esther said.

Estner disapproved of the friends.

"Female friends?" I said.

"No."

"How about Mr. Smith?"

"Only the young men."

"Young men?"

"Yes. He helped them. He was a, I don't know the word in English. *Mentor.*"

"Same in English," I said. "He mentors young men?"

"Yes. He is very generous. He helps poor boys to go to school and learn to do work and get ahead."

"And they came to his house?"

"Yes. He would teach them at his home."

"How about Mrs. Smith. She ever teach them?"

Esther was too nice to snort, but she breathed out a little more than normal.

"And why do you think she killed him?"

"For money."

"His inheritance?" I said.

"I don't understand."

"Money he would leave her."

"Yes."

"Was there a gun anywhere around the house?"

"I did not see one."

"Do you know anything I could use to prove that she killed him?" I said.

"She is a bad woman."

I nodded.

"Anything else?"

"Just what I have told you."

"Do you know anyone else who might have killed Mr. Smith?"

"No. It was she."

I finished the last of my coffee.

"This is very good coffee, Mrs. Morales."

"Would you wish more?"

"No. Thank you very much. I've kept you long enough."

Esther walked me to the door.

"She is a terrible woman," Esther said.

"Maybe she is," I said.

I thanked her again and left and walked back toward Codman Square past a dark blue Ford with its motor on, to the convenient hydrant where I had parked my car.

CHAPTER

FOURTEEN

Since she was a pillar of the community and adjudged not a flight risk, and because she had a dandy lawyer, Mary Smith was out on bail. So I could call on her in her home, rather than at the Suffolk County jail. It was nonetheless a daunting prospect. It was like talking to a dumb seventh-grader.

Rita Fiore let me in when I rang the bell. She was spectacular in a slim black and green polka-dot skirt and a bright green blouse.

"Mary asked me to sit in on your meeting," Rita said.

"Doesn't she get it that we're on the same side?" I said.

"I think she doesn't like to be alone with people."

"They might use a big word?"

"Kindness, now," Rita said. "Kindness."

We went into an atrium that looked over the small spectacular garden that someone maintained for Mary in the not entirely nourishing soil of Beacon Hill.

Mary stood when we came in. She was wearing high-waisted gray slacks and a white silk scoop-neck T-shirt. She was barefoot. A pair of black sling-back shoes were on the floor near the couch. One of them was upright. The other had fallen over.

"Oh, Mr. Spenser," she said, and put out her hand like a lady in a Godey print. "It is so lovely to see you. I mean it. It's really lovely."

"Gee," I said.

"Will you have coffee?"

"No thanks," I said. "I'm trying to cut back."

"Good for you."

"Brave," Rita said.

I ignored her.

"Mrs. Smith," I said. "Do you ever eat in a restaurant located in a store?"

"Louis'," she said. "They have a lovely cafe. I often have lunch there."

One point for DeRosa.

"Do you know a man named Roy Levesque?" I said.

"Who?"

"Roy Levesque."

"I don't think so."

"You went to high school with him. Dated him for a while, I believe."

"Oh, that one."

"Yes."

Mary sat, quiet and attentive and blank. It wasn't like talking to a dumb seventh-grader, it was like talking to a pancake.

"You still see him," I said.

Mary smiled and shrugged.

"Old friends," she said. "You know? Old friends."

"Whom you just a minute ago said you didn't know."

She smiled and nodded. I waited. She smiled some more. Rita crossed her legs the other way.

"Tell me about the young men that your husband, ah, mentored," I said.

Rita glanced at me. Mary smiled some more.

"He was so kind to them," Mary said. "He'd been a lonely little boy, I guess, and he wanted to make it easier for other lonely little boys."

"He give them money?" I said.

"Oh, I don't know. I really never had much to do with our finances."

"Help them out going to school? Maybe?"

"I'll bet he did," Mary said. "He was such a generous man."

"He'd not been married before?" I said.

"No. He was a confirmed bachelor," she said. "Until he met me."

"Do you know why?" I said.

"Why what?"

I took in some air. It was tinged with her perfume, or maybe Rita's, or maybe both.

"Do you know why he was a confirmed bachelor?"

"No."

She shook her head. Eager to please. Sorry that she couldn't supply more information.

"Do you know that he'd taken in a partner at the bank?"

"Oh no, I know nothing about the bank, or any of the other things."

"Other things?"

"Oh, I don't know." She laughed. "Nathan was always up to something."

"Do you know what they were?"

She shook her head.

"Are you sure you won't have coffee?" she said.

I shook my head. I was sure I needed a drink.

"Do you stay in touch with any other people from your high school days?" I said.

"Well, Roy."

"Anyone else?"

"Not really." She smiled again. "I've reached out to them, but they aren't, um, comfortable in my, ah . . ." She made a circular gesture with her hands.

"Circles," Rita said.

"Oh, yes, thank you. Sometimes I have such trouble thinking what I want to say."

"Lot of that going around," I said. "You know Felton Shawcross?"

"Felton? I don't think so."

"CEO of a company called Soldiers Field Development Limited."

"I don't really know anything about *companies*," she said.

"He was on the list of friends you had Larson give me."

"Oh, well, mostly Larson keeps that list. They are people who contribute money to things and when I have a big charity event, Larson invites them."

"So you don't know Shawcross?"

She shook her head sadly.

"Would Larson have consulted your husband on that invitation list?" Rita said.

I could tell she was getting bored. She didn't like being bored. Her voice had a small edge to it.

"I don't really know. They were certainly pals," she said. "They might have."

"Larson come to you through your husband?" Rita said.

Asking questions was better than sitting around crossing her legs.

"Yes," Mary said. "He's so really nice, isn't he?"

"Really," Rita said.

"How did he know your husband?"

"Oh God, I don't know. Some businessy thing."

Hard questions made her panicky. I moved on.

"Could you tell me how much your husband left you?" I said.

"Money?"

"Yes."

"Oh I couldn't possibly imagine," she said. "You'd have to ask Brink."

"Brink?"

"Yes."

"Who is Brink," I said.

"Our financial advisor."

"What would be his full name?" I said.

"Oh, I'm so used to him just being Brink. He's a really old friend."

"His name?"

"Brink Tyler. I think Brink is short for Brinkman."

"And where would I find him?"

"He's got an office in town here," she said.

"Under his own name?"

"No he works for a big company."

"Called?"

"Excuse me?"

"The name of the company," I said.

"Oh, Something and Something," she said. "I don't know." She frowned for a moment. "I have his phone number though."

"That would be fine," I said.

She stood gracefully and walked regally out of the room.

"I need a drink," Rita said.

"Right after we leave," I said.

Mary came back into the room with a pale green sheet of notepaper, on which she had written a phone number in purple ink. Her handwriting was very large and full of loops. I folded the paper and tucked it into my shirt pocket.

"Are you familiar with Marvin Conroy?" I said.

"Marvin?"

"Conroy," I said.

The little frown came back. She thought about the name.

"No," she said. "I'm really not."

We talked for a while longer. Mary remained eager and impenetrable. Finally neither Rita nor I had anywhere else to go. We thanked Mary and assured her that we were making good progress, which was a lie. We were making so little progress that I would have been pleased with bad progress. Mary walked us to the door and said she really hoped she'd been a help. We said she had, and left and went to the Ritz bar and had two martinis each. From our seat in the window I could see a black Lincoln Town Car, double-parked with its motor running, on Arlington Street.

CHAPTER FIFTEEN

Susan and I and Hawk and a woman named Estelle Raphael were having dinner at a place called Zephyr in the Hyatt Hotel on the Cambridge side of the Charles River. There was a lot of glass on the river side of the room and you could look at the river and across it and see the glare of a night game at Fenway Park.

They made many kinds of martinis here and would serve you a small sampling of three if you wished. Susan and Estelle both wished. Hawk and I stuck with the old favorite.

"I love how they look in the glass," Estelle said.

Hawk smiled and didn't say anything. Hawk could be comfortable not saying anything for longer than anyone I've ever known. Oddly his silence didn't make you uncomfortable. It was somehow natural to him. Susan was silent, too. That didn't make me uncomfortable either, but it wasn't natural to her. She had already drunk the first little martini, which was sort of a pale green, and had begun on the pink one. This, too, wasn't natural to her. Normally she would nurse those three little martinis for the night. It looked like the conversation was up to me and Estelle.

"You're a doctor?" I said.

"Yes. I run a fertility clinic in Brookline."

"Been running one of those most of my life," Hawk said.

"I know," Estelle said. "And it's fine work that you do."

The waitress came and took our order. Susan seemed not very interested in the menu. She said she'd have what I had. The black river glistened in the light sprawl from the city. I could see the Citgo sign, which had become famous solely by being visible behind the left-field wall at Fenway. To the right the gray towers of Boston University stuck up too high.

"You okay," I said to her softly.

She shook her head.

"Want to talk about it?"

She shook her head again.

"Want to go home?"

Shake.

I patted her thigh. She picked up the pink martini and finished it. There were tears in her eyes.

I said, "Hey." And put my arm around her shoulders. Probably the wrong move. She'd been holding it together before that. Now she began to cry. There was no noise. Just tears on her face and her shoulders shaking. I tried to pull her a little closer so she could cry against my chest. She didn't want to. We sat for a moment with my arm around her, patting her far shoulder.

"You like to be alone?" Hawk said.

Susan shook her head.

We were quiet. Susan took her napkin from her lap and wiped her eyes.

"Is my makeup fucked?" she said.

Estelle looked at Hawk. Hawk smiled.

"She coming out of it," he said.

"You look fine," I said.

"I'm sorry to be such a jackass," Susan said.

"Is there anything I can do?" Estelle said.

"No. Thank you."

"You want to talk?" I said. "You want to leave it be?"

"I don't want to talk," Susan said, "but I fear that I must. You can't suddenly burst into tears in the middle of dinner and offer no explanation."

"You can if you want to," I said.

Susan shook her head. "I lost a patient today," she said.

No one said anything. Estelle looked like she might, but Hawk put his hand on her thigh and she didn't.

"A boy, nineteen years old. He killed himself."

"Did you know he was suicidal?" I said.

"Yes."

"Are you feeling that you should have done more and better?"

"Of course."

"Do you know why he killed himself?"

"He was gay, and he didn't want to be," she said. "That's why he was seeing me. He desperately wanted to be straight."

"Isn't that a little outside the scope of your service?" I said.

As she talked she began to focus on the subject, as she always did, and in doing so she came back into control.

"It is hideously incorrect to say that one can help people change their sexual orientation. But in fact I have had some success, in doing just that."

"Helping gay people to be straight?" Estelle was startled.

"Or straight people to be gay. I've had some success doing both. The trick is over time to find out where they want to go, and where they can go, and try to achieve one without violating the other."

"I've never heard that," Estelle said.

She was genuinely interested, but there was that sound in her voice that doctors get which says, in effect, "If I haven't heard of it, it's probably wrong."

"No one is willing to incur the vast outrage that would ensue," Susan said.

"It's your experience," Hawk said.

"One ought not to have such an experience," Susan said. "And if one were stupid enough to have it, one should surely not talk about it."

"Shrinks, too," I said.

"Hard to believe," Hawk said.

"We've all known people who were married," Susan said, "and left the marriage for a same-sex lover. Why is it so impossible to imagine it happening the other way?"

"But who would be gay, if they could choose?" Estelle said.

"That is, of course, the existing prejudice," Susan said. "But it also implies that those who led straight lives could have chosen not to before they did."

Estelle didn't look too pleased about *existing prejudice,* but she didn't remark on it.

"I guess, as I think of it, that if a gay person entered into a straight relationship I'd assume it was only a cover-up."

"As if gay is permanent but straight is tenuous," Susan said.

"I hadn't thought of it quite that way before," Estelle said.

Susan nodded. "It's a hard question," she said.

"Kid making any progress?" Hawk said.

Susan smiled without pleasure.

"Yes. But it wasn't the direction he'd come to me looking for."

"He was discovering that maybe he wasn't going to change?" I said.

"Yes."

"You did what you could," Estelle said.

"I wonder if he'd have been better off without my help," Susan said.

"The rescue business is chancy," I said.

Susan smiled at me slowly, and patted my forearm.

"It is, isn't it," she said.

CHAPTER

SIXTEEN

Hawk was standing at the window of my office looking down at the green Chevy idling in front of Houghton Mifflin.

"Ain't it about time you and me pulled the plug on the followers?" Hawk said.

"Nope."

"How 'bout we go out to the Soldiers Field Development Corporation and shake up their boss?"

"Whom you believe to be Felton Shawcross," I said.

"Whom else?" Hawk said.

"CEO doesn't always know what his employees are doing," I said.

"True," Hawk said. "You and me for instance."

"My point exactly," I said.

"We could yank one of the followers out of his car and hit him until he tell us why he's following you."

"He may not know," I said.

" 'Cause he a employee," Hawk said.

"Yes."

"We could ask whom employs him."

"We can always do that. Just like we can always call on Felton Shawcross," I said. "Right now I figure if they wanted to make a run at me they would have by now."

"Probably."

"So they're just trying to keep tabs on me."

"Probably why they following you around," Hawk said.

"Because they want to know if I'm getting closer."

"Which they'll decide based on who you see."

"Whom," I said.

Hawk turned around and looked at me and smiled.

"So when you see somebody that's important, maybe they'll do something."

"Yep."

"And then ya'll gonna know whom is important."

"You're doing that *who/whom* thing on purpose, aren't you?" I said.

"Ah is a product of the ghetto," Hawk said. "Ah's trying to learn."

"And failing," I said.

"So it is your professed intention," Hawk said, "to continue visiting with principals in the case until you get a discernible reaction from those monitoring your movements?"

"That be my professed intention, bro," I said. "You be down with that?"

"Jesus Christ," Hawk said.

"I don't sound like an authentic ghetto-bred Negro?" I said.

"You sound like an asshole," Hawk said.

"Well," I said. "There's that."

CHAPTER

SEVENTEEN

Brinkman "Brink" Tyler had his office in a recycled warehouse on the recycled waterfront, not so far from the Harbor Health Club. I couldn't find an open hydrant, so I parked my car on the fourth level of the garage near the aquarium and walked, with Curly behind me looking intensely like he was just out for a walk. The Lexus that had been following me was pulled up across from me on the little side way that led to the aquarium. To my left the biggest urban renewal project in the country was chattering very slowly along, and corrupting all of the downtown traffic patterns in the process.

I found Tyler Financial Services on the lobby directory and took the elegant brass-and-rosewood elevator to the second floor. I could have found stairs, I suppose, but no one of stature would use them in this building. There was a lot of brick, and a lot of pickled oak, and a lot of hanging plants, and in Tyler's front office one crisp female secretary with a British accent. To her left a half dozen people were working in front of computer screens. To her right was a large office with an etched glass door. A discreet sign on the door said simply BRINK. I gave her my card and smiled her the smile that made me look just like Tom Cruise only bigger. She smiled back, though not very warmly. She seemed to sense that I wasn't a client. She checked her appointments, saw that I had one, and took me to the office door that said BRINK. She had a surprising amount of hip sway for one so crisp.

Brink Tyler was in full uniform: striped shirt, wide yellow suspenders, polka-dot bow tie. He looked to be maybe fifty, with a fresh haircut and a good tan. His hair was smooth.

"Brink Tyler," he said and put out his hand.

We shook firmly and I sat down. Behind Tyler was a huge picture window that overlooked the harbor, where the port of Boston activity was close by and frequent.

"You were Nathan Smith's broker," I said.

"What a shame. Yes, I was. And a personal friend as well."

"How was he doing?" I said.

"Excuse me?"

"How was his economic life?"

"Fine," Tyler said. "Excellent. Nathan was a member of a very old and successful family in this city."

"That's great, isn't it? Did he have a lot of money?"

"For God's sake, man, he owned a bank."

"Wow," I said. "Could I get a look at his monthly statements?"

"Oh, no. I'm afraid that's impossible."

"I represent his wife," I said.

"No, we'd really need her permission to show you that. She should have them. They went out only last week."

"She contends that she knows nothing, and only you, Brink Tyler, can answer my questions."

"My hands are tied," Tyler said.

"Call her," I said.

"Call her?"

"Yes. Ask her permission to give me the statements."

Brink wasn't thrilled with that. He sat back and thought about it. I sat back and waited. The blue stripes in his white shirt were wide. Tyler's cuff links were, or appeared to be, solid gold with a small design that I couldn't make out. Elegant.

"Well," he said. "I guess I could do that."

"Good for you," I said.

He picked up his phone and punched up a number without looking it up. He waited, talked briefly with Mary Smith, nodded several times, probably for my benefit, and hung up.

"No," he said.

"She won't authorize the statements?"

"No."

"She say why not?"

"No."

"And you didn't ask?" I said.

"It's her right," Tyler said. "She doesn't have to explain."

"How nice for her," I said. "You have any thoughts on who would want to kill Nathan?"

"I thought Mary did it."

"Because?"

"Because according to the paper the cops say she did it."

"And you believe it?"

"Sure. Why not?"

"She seem the type?" I said.

"Oh hell. I didn't know them like that. It was mostly a business friendship."

"So you think she murdered her husband, but you still need her permission to give me access to something as innocuous as his monthly statements?"

"I have a fiduciary responsibility here. I can't betray it. If I did, and word got around, who would trust me?"

"You're a stockbroker," I said. "You think people trust you now?"

"I don't think we have anything else to talk about," Tyler said.

"We do, Brink," I said. "But I'm willing to let it wait."

He didn't say anything. I got up and let myself out and, encouraged by her hip sway when she'd ushered me in, smiled my killer smile at the secretary. She smiled back at me pleasantly.

CHAPTER EIGHTEEN

When I got to the garage there was a fat guy lingering around the elevator, and Curly had come up quite close behind me. All three of us waited for the elevator. Curly and the fat guy were in competition to see which of them could look more nonchalant. When the elevator doors opened I turned and went past the two men and took the stairs instead of the elevator. Except in high-status buildings, elevators were for sissies.

I hotfooted it up the stairs and stopped on the fourth-floor landing. I could hear footsteps behind me. I went into the garage and walked toward my car. The fat guy was already there, exiting the elevator. Behind me Curly emerged from the stairwell. There was no one else in sight. The fat guy stepped in front of me.

He said, "Hold it there, pal."

I stopped. Behind me I could hear Curly's footsteps.

"You know," I said, "if you'd use the stairs every time, instead of taking the elevator, you wouldn't be so fat."

"Fuck you," the fat guy said.

"Gee," I said. "I hadn't thought of it that way."

I glanced back. Curly had stopped a few feet behind me. I did a half turn so that I could see both of them.

"We wanna know what you're doing," the fat guy said.

"Isn't it obvious," I said. "I'm talking with a couple of assholes."

"You're a funny guy," Fatso said. "Ain't he a funny guy, Bo."

"Funny guy," Curly Bo said.

"We ain't funny guys," Fatso said.

"I can see that," I said.

"And we want to know what you was talking to Brink Tyler about."

"Who?"

"You know who, you was just in his office."

"Oh," I said. "The Brinkster. Yeah. We were talking about diversifying my portfolio."

The fat guy didn't know what to say. He was used to people being scared of him, and it confused him that I wasn't. Also, he probably didn't know what a portfolio was. Bo, aka Curly, decided to step in.

"Okay, pal," he said. "Let's not fuck around here. We ask questions. You answer them, and you answer them straight. You understand? Or you get your ass kicked."

I spread my hands. "Hey," I said. "No problem. I didn't know you guys were serious."

"That's better," the fat guy said.

I kicked him in the crotch. While he was sinking to his knees, I swung around and popped Curly Bo with a right hook, and broke his nose. Bo was game. With the blood running down his chin he caught me with an overhand right on the side of the head. I hit him with a left hook and a right hook, and he went down. Fatso, on his knees and in pain, had fumbled a gun out. I kicked it out of his hand and heard it skitter away under one of the cars.

"You guys been roughing up civilians too long," I said. "Whatever you had to start with, you've lost."

"Fuck you," Fatso said.

Curly Bo was on his hands and knees, his head lolling, as he tried to clear the buzz from his brain.

"Who is it wants to know what I'm doing?" I said.

"Fuck you," Fatso said.

"Soldiers Field Development, perhaps?"

"Fuck you," Fatso said.

"Maybe I could beat it out of you," I said.

"Maybe you couldn't," Fatso said.

I stood for a minute and thought about it.

"You're right," I said. "Maybe I couldn't."

I went past them and got in my car and drove away. In the rearview mirror I could see them still on the ground as I turned onto the down ramp and headed out.

CHAPTER
NINETEEN

Rita had sandwiches and coffee sent in, and we ate lunch together at a cherry-wood conference table in her office. From where I sat I could look through Rita's big window and along the south shore to the narrow arch of land on which Hull dangled into the Atlantic.

"As I recall," I said, "when you were working in Norfolk County, you had an office with one wooden chair."

"And a view of my file cabinet," Rita said.

"And a lot of young male ADAs fresh out of law school hanging around the door with a clear interest in your body."

Rita smiled, and said, "Those were the days, my friend."

She took a small bite of her tuna-fish sandwich and chewed it in a ladylike manner, and swallowed gracefully.

"You ever sleep with a redhead?" she said.

"I'm not sure," I said.

"Lost count, have we?"

I had a ham and cheese sandwich on light rye. I ate some.

"Come to think of it," Rita said, "so have I."

I drank some coffee. "Good for us," I said.

"Yeah," Rita said. "Better than being able to remember the only one, in detail."

"There's only been one for a while," I said.

"I'm painfully aware of that," Rita said.

"Moving on," I said. "What did you find out about Soldiers Field Development?"

"Not a hell of a lot," Rita said. "They do real estate development—office buildings, motels, malls, stuff like that. Nathan Smith was on the board of directors."

"Oh ha!"

"Oh ha? What the hell is Oh ha?"

"Combination of *oh ho* and *ah ha*," I said. "I believe in variety."

"Me too," Rita said. "Do you say *oh ha* when you encounter a clue?"

"Or *ah ha*! Or *oh ho*! Depends on how many clues I have to react to."

"Well, it's not been much of a problem in this case," Rita said. "Why are you so interested in Soldiers Field Development?"

"There's been people following me since I took this case," I said. "They're connected to Soldiers Field Development."

"And now Nathan Smith turns up on the board," Rita said.

"Yes."

Rita smiled.

"Oh ha!" she said. "So how does this help my client?"

"If she didn't kill him, someone else did. I'm looking for the someone else."

"And how does this do that?" Rita said.

"I don't know yet," I said. "What I know is that something's going on with Soldiers Field Development that is connected to this case."

Rita picked up her coffee and stood and went to the window and looked out, sipping coffee.

"Are you thinking?" I said. "Or showing me your butt?"

"Both," Rita said. "I think better standing, but I haven't put in all those hours on the StairMaster to hide my butt under a bushel."

"The StairMaster has paid off," I said.

"Thank you. What do you think about the connection between a banker and a real estate developer?"

"It might involve money," I said.

Rita turned slowly and looked at me over the rim of her coffee cup.

"Wow," she said.

"It's magic, isn't it, how I can read people?"

"Magic."

"The bank is a family business," I said.

"That's what I'm told," Rita said.

"Has it always been just Smiths running it?"

"I don't know."

"Can you find out?" I said.

"Isn't that what we're employing you to do?"

"It's a waste of my talent," I said. "The premier law firm in Boston must have a dozen people who can research that faster than I can. But I'll bet none of them can take a punch."

"I haven't punched all of them," Rita said. "But I get your point."

"So, can you find out how many partners the bank has had?"

"That weren't family?"

"Yes."

"And you want to know this why?"

"Because he's got a partner now, guy named Marvin Conroy."

"You're suspicious of him?"

"Not really. But over the years I've learned to look for pattern so I can see variation, if any. Marvin Conroy might be a variation. If he is, I want to know why."

"Makes sense," Rita said.

"So can you do that?"

"Sure."

TWENTY

I leaned on the heavy bag and watched Hawk hit the speed. His face was expressionless, with a hint of amusement, the way it always was. He hit the bag with one hand, and then with both. He used his elbows. He appeared to be entirely relaxed, pleasantly absorbed in the music and movement of the bag.

"I'm going to drop in on Felton Shawcross," I said. "At Soldiers Field Development."

"Good," Hawk said without shifting his focus.

"Want to go?"

"Sure. They still tailing you?"

"Not unless they've gotten better at it."

"Figure Brink Tyler was the one they was worried about?"

"Yes."

"So now that you seen him they don't see no reason to follow you?"

"Maybe. Or maybe they are going to try another approach now that I've confronted the followers."

"So you going to go straight over there and present yourself, case they do want to take other measures."

"Yes."

"Which be why you inviting me along."

"Yes."

"We doing it to get even?" Hawk said.

"We're doing it because, right at the moment, I don't know what else to do," I said.

"There's a surprise," Hawk said.

An hour later, showered and dressed and looking like two million dollars each, we walked into the reception area of Soldiers Field Development and gave my name and asked for Felton Shawcross.

"A moment, please," the receptionist said.

She looked at Hawk as if hoping for his name, too. Hawk didn't respond. She excused herself and went through a door behind her desk and in a few moments came back along with a tall guy in a blue suit. He eyed Hawk as he approached.

"My name's Hatfield," he said to me. "What did you wish to see Mr. Shawcross about?"

"Nathan Smith," I said.

Hatfield frowned. "Who?"

"Hard name," I said. "Nathan Smith."

"Does Mr. Shawcross know Mr. Smith?"

"Doesn't everybody," I said.

Hatfield frowned again, and stood for a minute. He appeared to be thinking.

"I'll check with Mr. Shawcross," he said.

I nodded at the receptionist.

"I thought she already did that," I said.

"She checked with me," Hatfield said.

He had a thin sharp face. He looked formidable when he frowned. Which is probably why he frowned.

"And you are?"

"I'm the director of internal security," he said.

I looked at Hawk. He grinned.

"Internal security," he said.

"Wait here," Hatfield said and went back through the door behind the reception desk. Hawk and I went through it right behind him. He turned and started to say something. Hawk hit him with his left fist and Hatfield fell over backward. We were in a corridor. There were offices along the corridor. At the end of the corridor was a glass door that said FELTON SHAWCROSS in black letters. We went in. Shawcross was sort of a fleshy guy with his black hair slicked back. He was wearing a charcoal pin-striped suit and a black shirt with matching satin silk tie. His face was wide and his mouth was small under his big nose.

"What the fuck are you doing?" he said.

"I believe we are bursting into your office uninvited," I said.

He leaned back in his chair. "Where's Hatfield?" he said.

"My associate persuaded him to let us in," I said.

Shawcross nodded.

"Well," he said. "You're in. What do you want?"

Hawk leaned against the wall next to the door. I stood in front of the desk.

"Why are you worried about me talking with Brinkman Tyler?" I said.

"Tyler?"

"Tyler. You had people following me for days until I talked with Tyler, then they made a move on me."

"I didn't have anyone follow you," Shawcross said.

Behind me I heard people come through Shawcross's door. I glanced back. Hatfield was one of them. The right side of his face was already starting to swell. With him were three other guys in blue suits.

"Internal security," Hawk said.

I said, "You think?"

Hawk grinned.

"You all right, Mr. Shawcross?" Hatfield said.

"I'm fine," Shawcross said. "Before you throw them out, let's hear what these gentlemen have to say."

Hawk stayed by the door. The Internal Security Squad ranged along the wall on the other side of the room. I took a seat in a green leather chair with little brass studs showing on the face of the arms. I crossed my legs and admired my ankle for a moment.

"Nathan Smith has been murdered," I said. "His wife has been accused of the crime. I've been employed by her law firm to clear her."

"If she didn't do it," Shawcross said.

"I'm not sure the law firm cares," I said. "But I do. We don't have to be silly here, right? Since Nathan Smith is listed on your board of directors, we'll agree that you know him and since you are on his wife's invitation list we'll agree that you know her."

"Agreed," Shawcross said.

He was not a nervous guy. From their respective walls Hawk and the security squad were looking at each other.

"So as soon as I get hired onto this thing, I pick up a tail. My associate, Mr. Hawk, here, followed the tail back to this building. The tail was driving a car registered to this company."

Shawcross nodded, and said, "Um hm."

"I didn't do anything about the tail," I said. "Because I wanted to see if I could figure out why you were tailing me."

"It was not necessarily me," Shawcross said.

"Yesterday I talked with a guy named Brinkman Tyler, and after I finished, the tail made a pass at me."

"A pass?"

"They assaulted me," I said. "Wanted to know what I had talked with Tyler about."

"Really?" Shawcross said. "Did you tell them?"

"No."

"If you're trying to clear Mary Smith of her husband's murder, why are you talking to his broker?"

"Gotta talk to someone," I said. "Did you do any business with Nathan Smith?" I said.

"Business?"

"You develop real estate. He has mortgage money. He's on your board."

"It would be inappropriate for him to lend money to a business he was involved with," Shawcross said.

"How involved was he."

"Not," Shawcross said. "His presence on the board was a titular formality. But the bank regulators would frown on it nonetheless."

"So why have you been following me?"

"I know nothing of anyone following you. Do you know about that, Curtis?"

Hatfield frowned. It was harder now that his cheek was puffy, but he managed.

"No," he said. "I don't."

"Do your employees have access to the company cars?" I said.

"They're not supposed to," Shawcross said. "You know anything about this, Curtis?"

"No."

"I'm afraid I can't do much for you, Mr. Spenser," Shawcross said. "I'll certainly look into your charges, and inform you if we find anything substantial."

"I know you will," I said.

"In the meantime," Shawcross said, "should you feel inclined to barge in here again, you will be apprehended and held for the police."

"We're fairly hard to apprehend," I said. "Aren't we, Mr. Hawk."

"Heavens, yes," Hawk said.

"I don't intend to get into a pissing contest with you," Shawcross said. "I think we have nothing else to discuss."

"Until next time," I said.

No one else said anything as Hawk and I walked out of the office and down the corridor. As we passed through the reception area Hawk winked at the receptionist. She smiled.

CHAPTER

TWENTY-ONE

I was sitting in the guidance office at Franklin High School, talking with a sturdy gray-haired woman named Ethel Graffino.

"Mary Toricelli," she said. "Name doesn't ring a bell. A lot of students passed through here in thirty-five years."

"Class of 1989," I said. "Used to date a boy named Roy Levesque."

"Him I remember," Mrs. Graffino said. "He was in here a lot."

"Why?"

"Bad kid. Stole. Peddled dope. Cheated. Bullied any kids he could. I believe he dropped out without graduating."

"We all cheated," I said.

Mrs. Graffino smiled. "I know, but we're still required to condemn it."

"How about friends."

"Roy's? Or Mary's?"

"Either."

"I can give you class lists," she said.

"Two years on either side?"

" 'Eighty-seven through 'ninety-one? Are you going to harass these people?"

"No. I'm just going to ask them pleasantly about Mary and Roy."

"And you're trying to clear Mary of a murder charge?"

"Yes."

"And you are working for a law firm?"

"Yes. Cone Oakes."

"Is there someone I could call?"

"Sure." I gave her Rita Fiore's number.

She said, "Excuse me," called it and talked with Rita and hung up.

"I needed to be sure," she said.

She got up and went around to her office door and spoke to the secretary. Then she came back and sat.

"It'll only be a minute," she said. "Computers, you know, they've revolutionized record-keeping."

"I'm going to get one soon," I said.

"They're here to stay," she said.

Her phone rang. She excused herself again and answered. While she talked I thought how schools always felt like schools when you went in them. Even full grown and far removed, when I went in one I felt the old hostility again. While Mrs. Graffino spoke on the phone, the secretary came in with several pages of printout and put them on Mrs. Graffino's desk. She mouthed "thank you" to the secretary, pushed the printouts toward me, and nodded. I picked them up. Another list. About 1,200 names long. We never sleep.

CHAPTER
TWENTY-TWO

I sat with Susan and Pearl on the front steps of her big Victorian house in Cambridge, where she had her office on the first floor and her home on the second. I drank some beer. Susan had a martini I'd made for her, which she would sip for maybe two hours and leave half finished. Pearl was abstaining. People went by and smiled at us. Occasionally someone would walk a dog past, and Pearl would give a disinterested bark. Otherwise we were quiet.

"I should be wearing a sleeveless undershirt," I said.

"The notorious wife-beater undershirt," Susan said.

"Like Brando," I said. "In *Streetcar.*"

"Wasn't he a wonderful actor?" Susan said.

"No," I said. "I always thought he seemed mannered and self-aware."

"Really?"

"Can't help it," I said.

"But he was so beautiful."

"Didn't do much for me," I said.

A woman with shoulder-length gray hair walked by in hiking boots and short shorts. Her companion was tall and bald with a combover.

"How you feeling?" I said to Susan.

"Like I failed."

"The kid who killed himself?"

"Yes. I'm supposed to prevent those things."

"Didn't someone say something about the tyrannical 'supposed to's'?"

"Karen Horney," Susan said. "The tyrannical shoulds."

A guy walked past wearing a seersucker suit and one of those long-billed boating caps. He had a tan mongrel on a leash. The mongrel was wearing a red kerchief.

"Stylish," I said.

Susan nodded. Pearl lay between us on the top step with her head on her paws. The mongrel spotted Pearl and barked at her. Pearl's hearing wasn't much anymore. She glanced at the source of what must have been a dim sound, and growled a little without raising her head. Susan patted her absently.

"My office was the only place he was safe," Susan said. "His parents were appalled that he was gay. His schoolmates were cruel. He had no friends."

I didn't say anything.

"He could only be who he was in my office."

I nodded.

"I couldn't help him to change who he was. I couldn't help him to accept who he was. All I could accomplish, finally, for a few hours a week, was to provide a temporary refuge."

"Not enough," I said.

"No."

My beer was gone. I got up and went to the kitchen and got a jar of olives and another beer. I was trying Heineken again. A blast from the past. Susan was having another micro sip of her martini when I came back and sat down beside her. It was still warm, in the evening. The air had begun to turn faintly blue as the darkness came toward us. There was no wind. I plunked a fresh olive into Susan's martini. She smiled at me.

"If they have something somewhere," Susan said. "If they are loved at home. If they have a circle of friends. But if it's no good at home and it's no good at school . . . Goddamn it."

"No place to hide," I said.

"No place."

"Any theories why people are such jerks about it?" I said.

Susan shrugged.

"Nature of the beast," she said.

"There *is* a high jerk count among the general populace," I said. "Present company, of course, excluded."

Four girls from Radcliffe went past us in various stages of undress. They all talked in that fast, slightly nasal way that well-bred young women talked around here.

"Living in a college town is not a bad thing," I said.

Susan watched silently as the girls passed. She sipped her martini. I could hear her breathing.

"We are both in a business," I said, "where we lose people."

"I know."

"A wise therapist once told me that you can't really protect any-one, that sooner or later they have to protect themselves."

"Did I say that?"

"Yes."

"After you lost Candy Sloan?"

"Yes."

"I am wise."

"Good-looking, too," I said.

"But god*damn* it . . ." she said.

"Doesn't mean you can't feel bad when you lose one."

Susan nodded.

"Go ahead," I said. "Feel bad."

Susan nodded again.

"I've been fighting it," she said.

"And losing," I said.

"Yes."

"Give in to it. Feel as bad as you have to feel. Then get over it."

Susan stared at me for a while. Then she put her head against my shoulder. We sat for a time watching the street traffic. I listened to her breathing.

"That what you do?"

"Yes."

"Even after Candy Sloan?"

"Yes."

She fished another olive from the jar and put it in her martini. She had already drunk nearly a fifth of it.

"And," I said, "there's always you and me."

"I know."

A squirrel ran along Susan's front fence and up a fat oak tree and disappeared into the thick foliage. Pearl followed it with her eyes but didn't raise her head.

"You're a good therapist," Susan said after a while.

"Yes, I am," I said. "Maybe we should open a joint practice."

With her head still against my shoulder Susan patted my thigh.

"Maybe not," Susan said.

CHAPTER TWENTY-THREE

It took me three days to boil the class lists down to people I could locate, and another two days to find people on that list who remembered Mary Toricelli. One of them was a woman named Jamie Deluca, who tended bar at a place on Friend Street, near the Fleet Center.

I went in to see her at 3:15 in the afternoon when the lunch crowd had left and the early cocktail group had not yet arrived. Jamie drew me a draft beer and placed it on a napkin in front of me.

"I didn't really know her very good," Jamie said. "Mary was really kind of a phantom."

Jamie had short blond hair and a lot of eye makeup. She was wearing black pants and a white shirt with the cuffs turned back.

"What kind of a phantom?" I said.

"Well, you know. You didn't see much of her. She wasn't popular or anything. She just come to class and go home."

"Sisters or brothers?"

"I don't think so."

While she talked Jamie sliced the skin off whole lemons. I wondered if the object was to harvest the skin, or the skinless lemon. I decided that asking would be a needless distraction, and I had the sense that Jamie would find too much distraction daunting.

"Parents?"

"Sure, of course." Jamie looked as if it was the dumbest question she'd ever heard. "She lived with her mother."

"Father?"

"I don't know. When I knew her there wasn't no father around."

"Her mother still live in Franklin?" I said.

"I don't know."

"Her mother's name is Toricelli."

"Sure. I guess so."

"Who'd Mary hang out with?" I said.

"Most of the time she didn't hang with anybody," Jamie said. "She didn't have a bunch of friends. Just some of the burnouts."

"Burnouts?"

"Yeah. You know, druggies, dropouts, the dregs."

"Remember anybody?"

"Yeah. Roy Levesque. He was like her boyfriend. And, ah, Tammy, and Pike, and Joey Bucci . . . I don't know some of those kids. I think she just hung with them because she didn't have no other friends."

"Got any last names for Tammy and Pike?"

"Pike is a last name. It's a guy. I don't even remember his first name. Everybody called him Pike."

"How about Tammy?"

"Wagner, I think. Tammy Wagner. Kids used to call her Wags."

"You know where they are?"

"No. I moved in with my boyfriend soon as I graduated. Pretty much lost touch with the kids I knew."

"Boyfriend from Franklin?"

"No. Brockton. I met him at a club. He didn't last."

"Sorry to hear that."

"It's all right, he was a loser anyway."

"Lot of them around," I said, just to be saying something.

"Least he didn't knock me up," she said.

I nodded as I was glad about that, too.

"What was Mary like," I said. "Was she smart in school?"

"No. She was pretty dumb. Kids made fun of her. Teachers, too, sometimes."

"She ever get in trouble?"

Jamie shook her head and smiled.

"She was too boring to get in trouble," Jamie said.

The early cocktail crowd was beginning to drift in. The demands on Jamie made it harder to talk with her.

"Anything else you can tell me about Mary?" I said. "Anything unusual?"

Down the bar a guy was gesturing to Jamie. He had on a black shirt with the collar worn out over the lapels of his pearl gray suit.

"No," Jamie said as she started to move down the bar. "She was just a kind of dumb phantom kid, you know? Nothing special."

That would be Mary.

TWENTY-FOUR

I was in my office reading Tank McNamara and preparing to think about Mary Toricelli Smith some more when my door opened carefully and a woman poked her head in.

"Mr. Spenser?"

"Yes, ma'am."

She came in quickly and shut the door behind her.

"Remember me?" she said. "Amy Peters? From Pequod Bank?"

"Who could forget you," I said.

I gestured quite elegantly, I thought, at one of my two client chairs. She sat and crossed her legs, holding her purse in her lap with both hands. I smiled. She smiled. I waited.

"I . . . I . . . don't know quite how to do this," she said.

"I can tell."

"It's . . . I've been fired."

"I'm sorry," I said.

"It was . . . they said I had no business talking to you the way I did."

"What would be the business of a PR director?" I said.

She smiled and shrugged. "I don't even know what I said to you that was so bad," she said.

"Who exactly is 'they'?"

"Mr. Conroy. He called me into his office and questioned me quite closely about our conversation."

"And?"

"And when he was through he told me I was fired. The bank, he said, would give me two weeks' pay. But as of this moment I was through."

"What was the thrust of his questioning?" I said.

"He wanted to know what we talked about."

"Specifically," I said.

"He wanted to know what you asked about Mr. Smith, and what I told you."

"And why are you telling me?"

She stopped as if she hadn't thought about that before. I nodded encouragingly.

"I, well, I guess I thought it was important," she said.

"Un huh?"

"I mean, you are investigating his death."

"Do you have a theory about what the connection might be?" I said.

"They seemed pretty worried about you."

" 'They' being Marvin Conroy?"

"Yes."

"Why do you call him 'they'?"

"I don't know. I guess . . ." She paused and thought about my question. "I guess it's because I think there are people behind him."

"How so?"

"I think he has allegiances outside the bank," she said.

"Why do you think that?"

She was sitting very straight in her chair, sitting with her knees together, leaning forward from the waist. The position hiked her short skirt to mid thigh. I admired her legs.

"Well, he came in as a partner all of a sudden," she said. "This was a family-owned bank for more than a hundred years and all of a sudden here comes this man who's not a member of the family, and not, um, not of the social class you'd expect. And he wasn't in the bank much. When he was, he was . . . I don't know how to explain it. It's just an impression. But he was like some kind of court-appointed monitor, you know, like he was overseeing something."

"What social class is Conroy?"

"I don't mean he's what my mother would have called low class. But Mr. Smith was always so civilized and charming and gentle. He'd never fire anybody. He always made sure people were taken care of if they were sick or on maternity leave or anything. If there was an employee problem, he would call them into his office and talk it through with them."

"Conroy was a little less civilized?"

"He wasn't a dese, dem, dose kind of man. He was obviously educated. But he was very . . ." She searched for a phrase. "He was a bottom-line person. Very hard-nosed, no nonsense."

"Do you have an address for Conroy?" I said.

"Just the bank," she said.

"Okay. I'll go see him there."

"You won't tell him I spoke to you?"

"Not if you don't want me to."

"He's so . . ." She fluttered her hand. "He's so cold. He seems like someone who doesn't care about people."

"Does he frighten you?"

"Yes."

"It'll be our secret," I said.

She sat back, her body still straight, her knees still together. Both her feet were firmly on the floor, and she tugged the hem of her skirt slightly forward toward her knees. It was an automatic grooming gesture, like fluffing her hair. She probably didn't know she was doing it.

I smiled at her.

She looked at me.

"That's the other reason I came to tell you about this," she said.

"Which is?"

"That he frightens me."

I nodded.

"You seemed like someone to talk to if I'm frightened," she said.

I didn't have anything to say about that, so I smiled encouragingly.

"You seem like someone who would protect me," she said.

"Do you think you need protection?" I said.

"No, not really. I think I'm probably being a bit of a sissy."

"Anyone threaten you?"

"Oh, no, nothing like that. Conroy said I wasn't to talk of this matter, but he meant if I wanted a letter of reference for my next job."

I gave her my card. On the back of it, I wrote Hawk's name and cell phone number.

"If you feel threatened, call me, at any hour. If you don't reach me, call the number on the back. It's a large black man with his head shaved who could protect Australia if he were asked."

"Will he know who I am?"

"Yes."

"It's silly, of course. But I feel better knowing there's someone I can call."

"Anyone would," I said.

CHAPTER

TWENTY-FIVE

"Do you think she's in any real danger?" Susan said.

"Probably not," I said. "She's a bright young woman. Went to school, got an MBA, and this is the first time she's been fired."

"So her ego requires her to invest it with cosmic proportion."

"Once she's been fired a few times, she'll get used to it," I said.

"The voice of experience?"

"Something like that," I said.

I was cooking supper and Susan was pitching in by sitting at my kitchen counter drinking white wine and watching.

"Are you sure you're cooking those scallops long enough?" she said.

"Of what can we be sure," I said, "in this uncertain world?"

"We're not going to discuss the nature of being, are we?" Susan said.

"No."

"Thank God."

"Or whoever," I said.

"Stop that," Susan said.

She sipped her wine. I tossed the scallops in the sauté pan one more time and slid them onto a plate.

"They don't look cooked to me," she said.

"Suze," I said, "when you make tea, you burn the water."

"Do I hear you saying shut the fuck up?"

"At least about cooking," I said.

"Mum's the word."

I al dente'd the pasta and found it correct and poured it through a colander. I added some green peas and the sautéed scallops and tossed it all with some pesto sauce and put it on the counter. We ate at the counter, sitting side by side. Susan broke off a tiny piece from a loaf of French bread and ate it with a minimalist forkful of the pasta.

"You're right," she said. "You don't need my help."

"Not to cook," I said.

"Or much of anything else," she said.

I glanced at her sideways. "What about, you know?" I said.

"I don't consider that help," she said.

"Well, you are certainly not a hindrance," I said.

"Sometimes I think it's the only thing I'm good at."

I drank some beer. "Well, if there could only be one thing . . ." I said.

She didn't say anything. I could feel us drifting into a more serious corner of the evening.

"I can't get that kid out of my head," Susan said.

"The suicide?"

"Yes."

"Would you expect to, this soon after?"

"No," she said, "I suppose I wouldn't."

"In time," I said, "the sharp edges round off."

"I hope so."

"Seems a shame," I said, "that so harmless a variation should cause such pain."

"I know," Susan said. "People, especially young people, often think the circles they are in are the only circles that matter. They don't realize that there is a world where nobody much gives a goddamn."

Susan finished her wine. I poured her some more. She gestured me to stop at half a glass.

"It's not the condition," she said, "or whatever. It's the concealment."

"Like Watergate," I said. "It wasn't the burglary that caused all the trouble; it was the cover-up."

"Something like that," Susan said. "Pretending to be what you are not fills people with self-loathing. If they share their secret, even with a sex partner, then others have power over them. They are vulnerable to blackmail of one kind or another."

I carefully twirled some pasta onto my fork. Susan could eat with chopsticks, but she was nowhere at twirling pasta.

"You know," I said, "prior to Mary Smith, I cannot find any sign of a sex partner for Nathan Smith."

"How old was he when he got married?"

"Fifty-one," I said.

"Children?" Susan said. "With Mary?"

"No. But she told me that he was friendly with a number of young boys."

"Maybe you're looking for the wrong kind of sex partner," Susan said.

CHAPTER TWENTY-SIX

There was a photographer I knew named Race Witherspoon who was gayer than springtime and quite happy about it. He had his studios this year in a fourth-floor loft in South Boston, just across Fort Point Channel.

His studio was cluttered with tripods, and reflector umbrellas, and props, and Diet Coke cans. Curled Polaroid peel-offs were everywhere. A Flintlock musket leaned in a corner. A red feather boa was draped over the edge of an old rolltop desk. A cowboy hat lay on top of a file cabinet, a pair of combat boots stood side by side on an overturned milk carton. Light flooded in through a skylight. On the wall was a huge black-and-white blowup of two naked men. I tried to remain calm about it.

In the middle of the clutter Race was surgically immaculate. His white flannel pants were sharply creased. His turquoise shirt was fitted. His black-and-white shoes were gleaming.

"Oh my God!" Race said. "Man of my dreams."

"How unfortunate," I said.

"Well, honey," he said, "sooner or later they all come back."

"I need homo info," I said.

Race grinned and did a small shuffle ball change and spread his arms.

"You've come to the right place, Big Boy."

"If you were an older man," I said.

"Which I'm not," Race said.

"Certainly not," I said. "In all the years I've known you you haven't aged any more than I have."

"That's unkind," Race said. "But go ahead, if I were an older man . . ."

"Where would you be likely to go to meet young men?"

"How young."

"Boys."

"Nellie's," Race said. "Third floor. It's chickenfucker central."

"Joint in Bay Village?" I said.

"Nice turn of phrase, honey," Race said.

"I try to be appropriate," I said. "Bay Village?"

"Where else?"

"Ever go there?"

"Downstairs," he said. "I don't like children much."

I took the picture of Nathan Smith out and held it up for him. "Ever see this guy?"

Race examined the picture. "Not my type," he said.

"You know him?"

"No."

"If I took this picture down to Nellie's and showed it around, you think they'd tell me anything?"

"Nellie's doesn't stay in business by telling secrets," Race said.

"How about I pretended I was in your program?" I said. I shot out my right hip and put my fist on it.

Race said, "They could tell."

"How could they tell?"

"They could tell, honey."

"I'm not even sure this guy was gay," I said.

"And you're trying to decide?"

"I'm not trying to out him. He's been murdered."

Race nodded. "I'll tell you what, darlin'. You give me the picture. I'll find out for you."

I gave him the picture.

"Isn't there some saying about set a queer to catch a queer?" Race said.

"I think so," I said.

TWENTY-SEVEN

Frank Belson, with a fresh shave and his suit pressed, came into my office carrying two cups of coffee. He put one on my desk and sat down in a client chair and took a sip from the other one.

"Know a broad named Amy Peters?" he said.

"Yes."

"Tell me about her."

"Why?"

"Because I'm a cop and I'm asking you," Belson said.

"Oh," I said. "That's why."

Belson waited. I took the lid off the coffee and drank some. Belson was homicide and Amy Peters had been scared. There was a small sinking feeling in my stomach.

"She was until recently the vice president for public relations at the Pequod Savings and Loan which is headquartered in Cambridge."

"Why 'until recently'?"

"She got fired."

"For?"

"Talking to me."

"About what?"

"About a case I was on."

"Nathan Smith," Belson said.

"Yes."

"You doing anything for her?"

"No."

"How'd you know she was fired?"

"She came and told me."

"Why you?" Belson said.

"Why not me," I said. "What's up, Frank?"

"She's dead," Belson said.

The sinking feeling bottomed. Belson was looking at me carefully.

"We found your card in her purse," he said. "Nice-looking card."

"Thanks. How'd she die?"

"Bullet in the head. Looks self-inflicted."

"Her gun?"

"Unregistered. We're chasing the serial number."

"She didn't seem like somebody who'd have a gun," I said.

"You knew her?"

"Not really. Just talked with her a couple of times."

"About Nathan Smith?"

"Yes."

"Anything else?"

"She'd been fired. She seemed a little frightened of the guy who fired her."

"Marvin Conroy?"

"No grass growing under your feet," I said.

Belson ignored me.

"She want you to protect her?"

"Not really. Just consolation, I think. I gave her my card."

"And wrote Hawk's name and phone on the back," Belson said.

"Yes. I thought she might feel better if she had somebody to call."

"I guess she didn't," Belson said.

"No."

My office felt stuffy to me. I got up and opened my window a couple of inches to let the city air in. I looked out at Berkeley Street for a moment, looking at the traffic waiting for the light to change on Boylston.

"She leave a note?" I said.

"Yes. Said she was despondent over being fired."

"Authentic?"

"Hard to say. She left it on the computer."

"Technology sucks," I said.

Below me the light changed and the traffic moved across Boylston Street toward the river.

"Thing bothers me," Belson said.

I turned away from the window and sat down with my back to the air drifting in through the open window. I waited.

"Found a card for a lawyer in there in her purse where we found yours."

I waited.

"Ran that down before I came here. Woman lawyer. Says that Amy Peters was planning to sue Pequod for sexual discrimination for firing her."

"Which seems strange," I said, "if she was also planning to kill herself."

"Suicide's hard to figure," Belson said. "Women don't usually do it with a gun."

"What's the lawyer's name?"

"Margaret Mills. Firm is Mills and D'Ambrosio. You planning to help us on this?"

"Bothers me a little."

"She came to you scared and you sent her away and she ends up dead," Belson said.

"Something like that."

"Would bother me, too," Belson said.

TWENTY-EIGHT

I was in a booth in a donut shop talking to a gray-haired guy with a good-sized belly and a big mustache who had been for the last thirty years the youth service officer for the town of Franklin. His name was Pryor.

"His real name was Peter Isaacs," Pryor said. "Kids called him Peter Ike and it eventually became Pike."

"You remember him well?"

"Oh yeah," Pryor said. "Kid was a pain in the ass."

He took a paper napkin from the dispenser and wiped powdered sugar from his mustache.

"Wild-spirited?"

"Mean-spirited. Nasty little bastard. Did a lot of dope."

"He still around?"

"Yeah."

"How about Tammy Wagner?"

"She was his girlfriend," Pryor said. "Pike's. I don't know what happened to her."

"Joey Bucci?"

"Bucci . . . Yeah, sort of a faggy little kid, used to get bullied a lot. Hung with the burnouts because no one else would hang with him."

"You know where he is now?"

Pryor shook his head.

"No idea," he said. "He ain't around town."

"Where do I find Pike?"

"He's still here," Pryor said. "Works down the bowling alley. Sweeps up, cleans the rest rooms."

"Nice career choice," I said.

"Better than jail," Pryor said.

"Anything else you can tell me about Mary Toricelli?"

"No. Kind of a loser kid. The only reason I remember her is that she hung out with assholes like Isaacs and Levesque."

"You never got her for anything?"

"No. She was never into much. Just sort of dragged around after the hot shots. What'd she do, got a fast operator like you down here asking about her."

"Cops think she killed her husband," I said.

"Honest to God," Pryor said. "I didn't think she had the juice for it."

"I hope you're right," I said.

"So why do you want to talk to Isaacs?"

"See what he can tell me."

Pryor grinned. "Good thinking," he said. "You know what you're hoping to hear?"

"No."

"So how about if you hear it," Pryor said, "will you know it?"

"I hope so."

"Man, wait'll I tell the boys down at the station how I had coffee with a real private eye."

"You know how it goes," I said. "You get a case. You just keep poking around, see what scurries out."

"You get a case," Pryor said. "Currently I'm trying to catch the kids who spray-painted *fuck* on the middle-school front door."

"I guess you're not allowed to shoot them," I said.

"No," Pryor said. "They get to talk with a guidance counselor."

"How's that work?" I said.

"Keeps the guidance counselor employed," Pryor said.

I paid for the coffee. Pryor directed me to the bowling alley, and I drove on over to see Pike.

A couple of women in tight jeans and loose T-shirts were bowling candle pins in the first alley. The rest of the alleys were empty. The guy at the desk directed me to Pike, who was replacing the sand in the big free-standing ashtrays that stood near each lane. One of the women bowled a spare, and the clash of the pins echoed loudly off the hard surfaces. I showed him my license and we sat on one of the banquets where, when business was good, bowlers sat and waited for their turn.

Pike was a tallish guy with narrow shoulders and thinning blond hair that hadn't been cut. His face was red. When he sat next to me I could smell the booze on him.

"Jesus Christ, a fucking private detective? How about that? God-damn. You ever see that movie *Chinatown*?"

"What can you tell me about Mary Toricelli?" I said.

"You know, Jack Nicholson gets his nose cut, and he goes around with this fucking bandage on the whole freakin' movie."

"That's just what it's like," I said. "Mary Toricelli?"

"What about her?"

"What can you tell me about her?" I said.

"It worth any dough?"

"Maybe."

"Lemme see?"

I took a twenty out and showed it to him.

He grinned. "All right!" he said. "Whaddya wanna know?"

"Whatever you can tell me," I said.

"What if it ain't worth twenty?"

"Sitting there and saying nothing isn't worth anything," I said.

"So I may as well say something, huh?"

"May as well," I said.

One of the women rolled a strike. Both of them cheered and low fived each other.

"She turned out to be a lot better-looking than she was in school. You know? Sometimes that'll happen with a broad. She grows up and learns to take care of herself and turns out to be some pretty good-looking pussy."

"You've noticed that, too," I said.

"You should be talking to Roy Levesque. You know Roy?"

"We've met. Why I should I talk to him?"

"He still sees her."

"And you don't?"

"Well, I mean I see her in town sometimes," Pike said. "With Roy. But I mean Roy's *seeing* her, you know?"

"They intimate?"

"Oh sure, Roy's been fucking her for twenty years."

"I heard she was married," I said.

"Yeah, some rich guy. Never bothered her and Roy though."

"Was she going with Roy before she got married?"

"Sure."

"How'd Roy feel about her getting married?"

"He liked it. All that dough?"

"He get some of it?"

Pike looked at me like I'd asked about the Easter bunny. " 'Course he got some of it."

From the front desk the manager yelled at Pike. "Leagues start pouring in here at five," he said. "I need them ashtrays clean by then."

"Fuck you," Pike muttered but not so loud that the manager could hear him.

He stood and looked at me. "I gotta get to work," he said. "That worth twenty to you?"

I gave him the bill. He folded it over and stuck it in his pocket. Then he had a thought. I could tell he wasn't used to it.

"Hey, you're not gonna tell Roy I was talking about him, are you?"

"Why not?" I said.

"He don't like people talking about him. You gonna tell him, I'll give you back your twenty."

"Why doesn't he like people talking about him?"

"Roy's a mean bastard," Pike said. "You don't know what he's gonna do."

"What might he do?" I said.

"I just told you," Pike said. "You don't never know what he's gonna do."

From his shirt pocket he took a little nip bottle of vodka, un-screwed the cap, and drank it.

"Little cocktail," he said. "Settle my stomach."

"I won't tell Roy," I said.

TWENTY-NINE

"Did Amy Peters have a case?" I said.

"There's always a case," Maggie Mills said, "especially if you are one of a discriminated minority."

She was a senior partner at the law firm of Mills and D'Ambrosio, about fifty-five, and small, with crisp gray hair and hard blue eyes.

"Like women," I said.

"Women are a good example," she said. "It is nearly always possible to raise the issue of gender discrimination."

"Was it justified in this instance?"

Maggie Mills smiled. It was a somewhat frosty smile.

"That would need to be adjudicated," she said. "Clearly there was something at issue besides her professional competence."

"Why do you say so?"

"Among other things, she was frightened," Maggie Mills said.

"I know. Do you think she came to you because she was scared?"

Maggie Mills shook her head briskly.

"She came to me because her ego couldn't take it," Maggie Mills said. "She couldn't stand being fired."

"Did you gather she was afraid of her boss?"

"I didn't gather anything," Maggie Mills said. "She didn't speak of it. But I have been in business for a long time, and I can recognize a frightened woman."

"You have any reason to think she was suicidal?" I said.

"The police asked me the same thing," Maggie Mills said. "And I'll answer you the same thing I answered them. I'm an attorney, not a psychiatrist. I don't know what someone is like when they are suicidal. But it seems odd to me, personally, that she would hire a lawyer and then kill herself."

"At least until the bill came."

"The death of a young woman should not evoke levity," she said.

"One of my failings," I said, "is finding levity where it doesn't belong."

"What is your interest in the case?"

"It may be pertinent to another case I'm working on," I said.

"Do you have any other interest?"

"She came to me and told me she was sacred and I reassured her."

"And you are now reconsidering that?"

"It would have been nice if I'd done something useful."

Maggie Mills studied me for a time. "So her death is not solely an occasion for levity."

"Not solely," I said.

"I didn't help her either," Maggie Mills said.

I nodded.

"It seems that both of us might have failed her."

"Seems possible," I said.

"It is my intention to continue to look into the gender discrimination matter," Maggie Mills said.

"Even though your client is dead."

"The crime didn't die with her," Maggie Mills said. "If either of us discovers anything, perhaps we could share it."

"I'm already employed by Cone Oakes," I said.

"This is not a professional matter," Maggie Mills said. "This is personal."

"Yes," I said. "It is."

CHAPTER THIRTY

It was Marvin Conroy's turn. No one at the bank knew where he was. His ferocious-looking secretary knew only that he wasn't there. She had no idea where he was. On my way out I picked up a copy of the bank's annual report and took it with me. I found it difficult to believe that no one at the bank knew where the CEO was, so I went and sat in my car across the street and looked at the report. In the front was a big picture of Nathan Smith and, on the facing page, a big picture of Marvin Conroy. He looked as if someone had advertised for an actor who looked like a chief executive. Square jaw, receding hair, clear eyes that looked right through the camera lens. I put the report aside with Conroy's picture up, and waited.

At 2:15 he came out of the bank and walked down First Street, toward the Cambridge Galleria, a big shopping center that backed up onto the old canal. This part of Cambridge wasn't one where a lot of people walked, and I had to let him get pretty far ahead of me to keep from being obvious. But Conroy wasn't looking for a tail. He was a big guy with a good tan and an athletic stride. He was balder than his picture indicated, but he made no attempt to conceal the fact, wearing his hair very short. It looked like he went to a good barber.

He went into the Galleria with me behind him and walked straight to the food court. He stood in line for a meatball sandwich and a large Coke, and when he got it took it to an empty table. It was a standard shopping-center food hall with maybe fifteen fast food outlets surrounding an open area full of small tables. The patrons were mostly adolescent kids, as was the service staff.

I'd been hoping we'd end up at an elegant club that catered to CEOs. But experienced detectives are flexible. I bought a cup of coffee and went over and sat down at his table with him. He glanced up at me, looked around at the number of empty tables still available, and looked back at me with a frown.

"Do I know you?" he said.

"This is very disappointing," I said. "The CEO of a multibranch bank and you're eating in the Galleria food court."

"Cut the crap," he said. "Who the hell are you?"

He had a very cold gaze. There was something cruel about the way his forehead sloped down over his little sharp eyes, something about the aggressive jut of his prominent nose, and the thickness of his wide jaw.

"Who are any of us," I said. "Why'd you fire Amy Peters?"

"What?"

"It was a two-part question. I raised the metaphysical question about human identity, and the more worldly question of why you fired Amy Peters."

"What the hell business is it of yours?"

"Human identity is a concern to us all," I said.

"Goddamn it, I'm talking about Amy Peters. Why are you asking me about her?"

"Amy Peters is dead," I said. "I want to know why."

A couple of teenaged kids passed by wearing baggy jeans and do-rags. They each had a tray of french fries and a giant Coke. I wondered if there were such a thing as negative nourishment.

"Are you a policeman?" Conroy said.

I gave him my most coppish deadpan stare.

"What was she fired for?" I said.

"I know nothing of her death," Conroy said. "She was fired because she was incompetent."

"She was bringing suit against you for gender discrimination."

"Of course she was. They all do. You fire somebody and it's suddenly un-American."

"Can you tell me about her incompetence?"

Conroy leaned back in his chair a little, and gave me a hard CEO look.

"I guess I'd better see some identification," he said.

"Amy Peters told me she was fired because she talked to me."

"You're that fucking private detective," Conroy said.

I smiled at him.

"I am he," I said.

Conroy stared at me and opened his mouth and thought about what he was going to say and decided not to say it and closed his mouth. Then he thought of something else.

"Fuck you," he said.

He stood abruptly and walked through the food court and out into the mall. I got up and strolled into the mall after him. At the far end I saw Vinnie Morris come out of a music store wearing a Walkman and earphones. He went out through the mall door onto the street ahead of Conroy. After Conroy went out, Hawk stopped window-shopping and drifted out after him.

THIRTY-ONE

"You seem down," I said to Susan. "Would you like me to have sex with you and brighten up your week?"

She shook her head. We were at a small table in the high-ceilinged bar at the Hotel Meridien. I had beer. Susan was barely touching a cosmopolitan.

"That's the answer everybody gives me," I said.

"The parents of the boy who committed suicide are suing me," Susan said.

"They blame you," I said.

"Yes."

"I guess they'd probably have to," I said.

"I know."

"You've seen a lawyer?"

"I talked with Rita."

"Rita? I thought you didn't trust Rita."

"I don't trust her with you," Susan said. "I think she's a good lawyer."

"She is," I said. "And a big firm like Cone Oakes has a lot of resources."

Susan smiled without much pleasure. "So I'm employing Rita," Susan said. "And she's employing you."

"What's she say about the lawsuit?"

"She feels it's groundless."

The Hotel Meridien was in a building that had once been a bank. The bar was in a room where they probably used to keep the money. The ornate ceiling looked fifty feet high.

"How do you feel?"

"I feel guilty."

I ate a few peanuts. Eating a few peanuts was not easy. Mostly, I tended to eat them all.

"Be surprising if you didn't," I said.

"I know. I know the guilty feeling comes from my reaction to the event. Not the event itself."

"Still feels bad, though," I said.

"Yes."

I ate a few more peanuts, and determined to eat no more. The waitress brought me a second beer. Susan took in a milligram of her drink.

"You know what makes me love you?" she said.

"My manliness?"

She smiled.

"You haven't tried to talk me out of feeling guilty," she said.

"Be aimless," I said.

"Yes. But not everyone would know that."

"It's a gift," I said.

I could almost see Susan decide that she had been down as much as she was prepared to be.

"Tell me about what's going on in that case you're working on for Rita."

"It keeps spreading out on me," I said. "The more I investigate, the more I learn. And the more I learn, the more I don't know what's going on."

"That happens to me often in therapy," Susan said. "I know something's in there in the dark and I keep groping for it."

"That would be me," I said. "Groping."

"What do you know?"

"I know that Smith is dead. I know that I talked to a woman at his bank and she got fired and now she's dead."

"How did she die?"

"Appears to be suicide," I said.

"But?"

"But she had just been to a lawyer about a gender discrimination lawsuit against the bank," I said.

"So why would she be making long-range plans just before killing herself?"

"Yes."

"It happens sometimes," Susan said. "It is an attempt to convince themselves of the future."

I shrugged and had a Brazil nut that I plucked out from among the remaining peanuts. One Brazil nut wouldn't hurt anything.

"The bank was a family-owned business, until Marvin Conroy came aboard. He fired the woman for incompetence. And he doesn't want to talk with me. I know that some people from Soldiers Field Development Limited are interested in what I'm doing and want me to stop doing it. I talked with Smith's broker and was assaulted shortly thereafter."

"Assaulted?"

"Yeah. They weren't very good at it."

"That's nice," Susan said.

"DeRosa, the guy that says Mary Smith wanted him to kill her husband, is represented by Ann Kiley, Bobby Kiley's daughter."

"The defense lawyer?"

"Yes. The firm is Kiley and Harbaugh, but it's really Kiley and Kiley. Father and daughter."

"That's sort of charming," Susan said.

"It is," I said. "But why is a firm like that representing a stiff like DeRosa?"

"Social conscience?"

"You bet," I said. "And then we have Mary Smith herself. She still seems to have a relationship of some sort with an old high school boyfriend who is evasive when asked about it."

"By you."

"By me."

"And what did he say?"

"As I recall," I said, "he told me to 'shove fucking off.' "

"She must have been attracted to him by his silver tongue," Susan said. "What does Mary say?"

"You'd have to talk with Mary to understand," I said.

"Why? What's she like?"

I found another Brazil nut in the dish, and a cashew. I ate both of them. I hadn't seen the cashew before.

"She's a living testament to the power of dumb."

"Meaning?"

"Meaning you ask her something and she seems too dumb to answer it. You can't catch her in contradictions because she doesn't seem aware of them even after they're pointed out."

"Seems kind of smart to me," Susan said.

"I don't think so," I said. "I think she knows she's dumb and sort of uses it."

"Maximizing her potential," Susan said. "Anything else bothering you?"

"Yeah. Nathan Smith. He was unmarried until he married Mary, in his fifties. According to Mary, he was a friend and helper to a number of young men, both prior to and during his marriage to her."

"If he were gay, would he have hidden it? This is not a closeted age."

"Old Yankee family. President of the family bank."

"Still," Susan said.

"Remember your patient," I said.

"He was a boy. And he was very troubled."

"Nathan Smith was once a boy."

Susan nodded.

"Of course," she said.

"It's something I've got to look into."

"Because you think it would have bearing on his death?"

"Suze, I don't have a goddamned clue what has a bearing on his death. Every time I find a rock I turn it over."

We sat quiet for a time. She held her partially sipped cosmopolitan in both hands, looking at its pink surface.

"It bothers you that the woman from the bank died."

"She came to me and told me about getting fired," I said. "She said she was afraid of Conroy, the new CEO."

"And you feel you should have protected her?"

I shrugged.

"So." Susan's eyes were very big as she looked up at me over the glass. "You're feeling a little guilty, too."

"Yep."

"And, like me, you know that it's not rational."

"Just like you," I said.

"I think you've never quite altogether forgiven yourself for that woman in Los Angeles all that time ago."

"Candy Sloan," I said.

Susan nodded.

"Only time I ever cheated on you," I said.

"Makes it that much worse, doesn't it?" Susan said.

"I'm not sure it makes any difference," I said.

Susan smiled the smile she used when she knew I was wrong but planned to let me get away with it.

"It's frustrating to have so many questions," Susan said.

"It gives me a lot of handholds," I said. "I keep groping long enough I'll get hold of an answer."

"Yes," Susan said. "You will."

"You too," I said.

Susan smiled at me.

"We persist," she said.

The waitress came to ask if we needed anything. Susan shook her head. I ordered another beer.

"And another bowl of nuts," I said.

CHAPTER

THIRTY-TWO

Race Witherspoon opened his studio door for me looking as if he had just ingested a fat canary. He had the collar of his silk shirt turned up and the brim of a summer straw hat tilted forward over his eyes.

"You're wearing your hat indoors," I said. "Is it a gay thing?"

"Race Witherspoon," he said. "Super sleuth."

"I gather you have information for me," I said.

Race sat down in a client chair facing me and crossed one leg over the other. He had on knee-length black shorts and dark leather sandals.

"Nice pedicure," I said.

"How sweet of you to notice, bubeleh."

"Years of training," I said.

"Nathan Smith was a serious chickenfucker," Race said.

"How nicely put," I said. "He was drawn to young boys?"

"Early adolescent when he could get them," Race said.

"How solid is this?"

"Honey," Race said, "I talked with some of the chickens."

"He give them money?"

"Yes, but not like it sounds. He was more like a fairy godfather." Race grinned. "So to speak. He'd pay for dance lessons or music lessons or whatever. He set up scholarships for them to go to college. Paid for counseling. Wish I'd met the dear man when I was younger."

"So you could have gotten counseling?" I said.

Race snorted.

"How out was he?" I said.

"Way in the back of the closet, darlin'. Told people at Nellie's his name was Marvin Conroy."

"Marvin Conroy?"

"Un-huh. Nice butch name."

"Nice butch guy," I said. "Nathan had a sense of humor."

"So he borrowed some straight guy's name," Race said.

"Yes."

"Bet the straight guy wouldn't like it."

"No."

"Another thing," Race said. "One of the bartenders at Nellie's told me that somebody else had been in a year and a half ago asking about the same guy."

"Nathan Smith?"

"Un-huh, aka Marvin Conroy."

"The bartender know who this was?"

"Nope, just a middle-aged straight white guy."

"How could he tell he was straight?"

"Gay-dar," Race said. "You wouldn't understand, sweetie."

"The bartender remember what the guy looked like?"

"Just what I said."

"What did the bartender tell him?"

"Nothing. I told you, Nellie's doesn't stay in business by telling on their clients."

"Is he sure about the time?" I said.

"It was right after the Super Bowl," Race said. "The one where the Rams won."

"People at Nellie's watch the Super Bowl?" I said.

"All those muscle men in tight pants?" Race said. "All that butt patting? Honey, get real."

"I never thought of it that way," I said.

" 'Course you haven't," Race said. "You're much too straight."

"Unfortunately," I said, "I'll think of it now every time I watch football."

"It's good to have a queer perspective now and then," Race said. "How's Susan?"

"As always," I said, "beautiful and brilliant."

"Hot, too."

"You think?" I said.

"Hot, hot, hot," Race said. "If I was ever going to jump the fence . . ."

"But you aren't," I said.

"Oh, God, no!" Race said.

"Whew!"

CHAPTER THIRTY-THREE

It was early evening when I left Race's loft. Darker than it should have been, because it was overcast, with a warm rain falling on A Street. I turned up the collar of my raincoat and walked toward my car, which was parked past the overpass, toward Summer. There was no traffic. In the soft damp hush I thought I heard a car engine idling, but couldn't tell which one it was. On my left ahead, beneath the underpass, was an iron stairway that led down from the street above.

I paused. I had annoyed a lot of people in the last week or so. If someone wanted to shoot me this would be a dandy spot. Come down the stairs behind me, put a bullet in the back of my head, get into the car waiting at the curb, be out of sight in ten seconds. I stood. Nothing happened. I wasn't even sure I had heard the engine idling. And even if I did, people sat in cars with engines running all the time. Air conditioner on. Waiting for the wife. Listening to the radio. Calling on the car phone. I was probably overreacting. Other than embarrassment and time wasted, however, there was no down side to overreacting. Underreacting might get me killed.

I took my gun out and held it against my side, and walked under the bridge. The iron stairs were on my left, and as I passed them, I turned suddenly and ran up them. Three steps from the top I collided with a guy coming down. He had a gun in his hand and when I ran into him, it went off over my left shoulder. I shot him. He made a soft grunt and fell backward and down onto the wet iron stairs. I turned and ran down the stairs toward the street. Behind me I could hear the body slide down a couple of stairs.

As I reached the street, headlights caught me and a maroon Chrysler pulled out from the curb behind where mine was parked. I dove flat onto the sidewalk at the foot of the stairway and heard a burble of gunshots rattle against the stone bridge buttresses. Automatic weapon. As the car ripped down A Street, its wheels spinning on the wet surface, I got my feet under me and headed back up the stairs. The car did a screeching U-turn and headed back. I stepped over the body of the guy I had shot. His gun lay two steps above him on the metal stair tread. It was a Glock. Below me the car slowed and someone sprayed the area at the foot of the stairs with gunfire. I went to the edge of the overpass and fired straight down into the roof of the car beneath me. The Chrysler lurched once, then surged forward and headed out of sight toward Congress Street, leaving a smell of burnt rubber and gunpowder to mix with the wet smell of the rain, and the more distant smell of the harbor.

I reloaded my gun and went back down the iron steps and knelt beside the man I'd shot. He'd been a tall, young guy, wearing a green satin warmup jacket with *Paddy's* in white lettering across the front, broken between the D's by the snap front of the jacket. His freckled face was blank now, wet with the rain. His eyes were empty. My bullet had caught him under the chin and plowed up through his brain and out the back of his head. There was a rain-diluted splatter of blood and tissue on the step where he'd fallen. He still wore his Red Sox cap.

In his pants pocket I found a spare magazine for the Glock, and two twenty-dollar bills folded over twice. No wallet. No identification. If anybody in the vicinity of Fort Point Channel had heard the gunfire they had ignored it. There was no activity on the street. No sirens. Just the merciless rain, and me.

I put my gun back in my holster and went down the stairs to my car and called the cops.

CHAPTER

THIRTY-FOUR

I got through with the cops about 3:30 in the morning. During which time I drank too much coffee. The license plate on the Chrysler had been stolen earlier in the week from a 1986 Chevette, which belonged to an elderly woman in Amesbury. None of the cops recognized the kid I'd killed. The ME promised fingerprints by tomorrow night. Belson told me they'd probably need to talk to me some more, but there was nothing wrong with my story, and he couldn't see any charges being brought. I agreed with him.

At 4:15 I was lying on my back in my bed, exhausted and wide awake. I had killed people before, and didn't like it. I'd also had too much coffee. The way the kid's face had looked with the pleasant summer rain falling on it made me think of Candy Sloan's face, lying in the rain among the oil derricks, a long time ago. Susan was right. I had never quite put that away.

It was daylight before I got to sleep. I slept and woke up and slept and woke up until 2:30 in the afternoon, when I dragged out of bed, logy with daytime sleep. I took a shower and put on my pants and went to the kitchen, acidic still with too much really bad coffee. I made myself a fruit smoothie with frozen strawberries and a nectarine. I poured the smoothie into a tall glass and took it with me to the living room and sat in a chair by the window and looked out at Marlborough Street and drank some.

The soft rain of the night before had turned harder. It was dark for midafternoon and everything was gleaming wet. Cars were clean. The leaves on the trees were fat and shiny with rain. Good-looking women, of which the Back Bay was full, moved past now and then, alone, or walking dogs in doggie sweaters, or pushing baby strollers protected by transparent rainproof draping. The women often had bright rain gear on, looking like points of Impressionist paint in the dark wet cityscape. My apartment was quiet. I was quiet. The rain was steady and hard but not noisy, coming straight down, not rattling on the window. I sipped my smoothie. My doorbell rang.

I picked up my gun off the kitchen counter and went and buzzed the downstairs door open. And went and looked through the peephole, after a moment. The elevator door opened and Hawk stepped out. I opened the door and he came in, wearing a white raincoat and a panama hat with a big brim. And carrying a paper bag. I knew he saw the gun. He saw everything. But he had no reaction.

"Raspberry turnovers," he said.

I closed the door. He held out the bag, and I took a turnover. I ate it while I made coffee and Hawk hung up his coat and hat.

"Been following your man Conroy," Hawk said.

He stirred some sugar into his coffee.

"He make you?"

"Me?" Hawk said. "Vinnie?"

"I withdraw the question," I said.

Hawk took a turnover from the bag and ate some. I sipped some coffee. It didn't feel so bad. It sat sort of comfortably on top of the smoothie.

"We picked him up where you left him," Hawk said.

I nodded.

"I saw you," I said.

" 'Cause you looking for us."

"Sure."

"So me and Vinnie, we double him, me on foot, Vinnie in the car. And he never knows we there. He goes back to the bank. Stays about an hour, then comes out and gets his car. I hop in with Vinnie and we tail him up to Boxford."

"Long ride," I said.

"Yeah. Deep into the fucking wilderness," Hawk said. "Vinnie kept him in sight."

"Vinnie's good at this kind of work," I said.

"He is," Hawk said.

"But is he fun, like me?"

"Nobody that much fun," he said. "You like these turnovers?"

"Yes."

"Place in Mattapan, make the crust with lard, way it's supposed to be made."

"That would make them illegal in Cambridge," I said.

"So Conroy drives to a house in Boxford," Hawk said, "and parks in the driveway and gets out and goes in, and me and Vinnie sit outside, up the street a ways, and wait."

I got a second turnover out of the bag and started on it. Lard. Hot diggitty!

"How long he in there," I said.

"He don't come out," Hawk said. "Lights go out about eleven-thirty. 'Bout two in the morning we decide maybe it's over. So I go check out the house. No name on the door. No name on the mailbox. There was a car in the garage, but I couldn't see the license plate."

"So you came home," I said.

"Yep. Left Vinnie at the bank, pick him up when he come in for work."

"What was the address up there?" I said.

"Eleven Plumtree Road," Hawk said. "In a big honky development."

"How do you know it's honky?" I said.

Hawk chewed some turnover and swallowed and smiled at me.

"Boxford?" he said.

"Good point," I said.

CHAPTER

THIRTY-FIVE

It was still raining when I drove up Route 95 to Boxford. It was early evening, after the commuter traffic had dissipated. It was maybe twenty-five miles north of Boston, where the city seemed a safe distance and there were cows. I turned off at Route 97 and plunged into the wet green exurban landscape.

Plumtree Road was the way into a big two-acre zoned development of expensive white houses with two-car garages and a lot of lawn. Hawk had been right. It was just the kind of place that affluent Anglo-Saxons seemed unable to resist.

Number 11 was just like number 9 far to its left, and number 13 far to its right, except that the shutters at number 11 were dark green. The front lawn that sloped to the street was undulant and wide. There were expensive shrubs along the foundation, which would someday grow and be beautiful. But now, like the rest of the development, they were too new. I pulled into the wide, gently curving driveway and parked in front of the big green doors of the two-car garage.

The lights were on in the house. I walked up the blue slate stepping-stones to the front door and rang. I was wearing my black Kenneth Cole microfiber waterproof spring jacket and my navy Boston Braves hat with a red bill. Anyone would be thrilled to find me standing on their front step at 7:15 on a rainy evening. The door opened and a good-looking blond woman in white shorts and a jade-green tank top looked at me. She did not seem thrilled. And I thought I knew why. It was Ann Kiley.

"Yes?"

"Ann Kiley," I said.

"Yes?"

I was completely out of context. She had no idea who I was. I tipped my Braves cap back from my forehead. I smiled warmly.

"It's me," I said.

She stared at me.

"So it is," she said finally. "What do you want?"

"I want to come in out of the rain," I said. "And talk about Marvin Conroy."

She didn't blink, just looked at me for another ten seconds, then stepped away from the door. "Come in," she said.

I went in and took off my hat, as my father and my uncles had always insisted I do when I went indoors. I was in a big entry foyer that opened into what looked like a very large living room.

"I was about to have a cocktail," Ann Kiley said. "Would you care for something?"

"I would enjoy a big scotch and soda if you have it."

"Certainly," she said. "Hang your coat in the front hall closet."

I did as instructed and followed her into the living room. She pointed me toward a big tan leather armchair with a matching hassock, and crossed to the bar. She made me a scotch and soda and herself a martini, brought me my drink, and sat down on the couch across the room and tucked her bare feet up.

"First one of the day," she said and took a sip and smiled. "Always the best one."

I sipped my scotch, and nodded.

"You're right," I said. "Tell me about Marvin Conroy."

She didn't flinch. She sat perfectly still with her martini and met my look. She had great eyes, not as great as Susan's, but just as well made up, and there are degrees of greatness.

"What do you wish to know?" she said.

That was good. No *who's-martin-conroy?* She had already understood that if I didn't know something I wouldn't be asking about him. Evasion would make it look worse. So she did the best she could in a difficult circumstance.

"A pleasure to observe a good legal mind," I said. "You've remained noncommittal and your question puts it back on me. The more I say, the more you'll know what I know."

She smiled to acknowledge the compliment and sipped her martini. Neither of us said anything for a moment.

"My problem," I said finally, "is that I don't know what I wish to know."

She nodded and was quiet.

"So I'll tell you what I do know," I said.

I took another pull on my drink. She'd made it well. A lot of ice, the proper balance of scotch with soda. Be nice to drink several of them with her. I leaned back a little and put my feet up on the hassock.

"Here's what I know. Marvin Conroy is an executive at Pequod Savings and Loan, which was Nathan Smith's bank and had been in the family since before Pocahontas. When I went to ask about Smith's death, I talked to a PR woman named Amy Peters, who is now dead. Conroy refused to talk about it. After I talked with him, some people tried, unsuccessfully I might add, to kill me."

Ann Kiley cocked her head a little as if she were glad to hear I hadn't died.

"You represent Jack DeRosa, who says Mary Smith asked him to kill Nathan Smith. So both you and Conroy are connected to Nathan Smith in some way."

"Six degrees of separation," Ann murmured.

Her drink was gone. So was mine. She got up, collected my glass, went to the bar, and mixed us each another drink.

"Last night," I said, "Marvin Conroy came here and spent the night."

Ann Kiley smiled again without meaning anything by it. I waited. She waited. I waited longer.

"And your question?" she said.

"Was it good for you, too?" I said.

"Don't be offensive."

"Part of my skill set," I said. "What can you tell me that will help me with my work?"

"And your work is?"

"To find out who killed Nathan Smith."

"Even if it's his wife?"

"Even," I said.

"I was under the impression you were hired to clear her," Ann said.

"What's the connection between you and Conroy and Smith and DeRosa?"

"The connection between me and Marvin Conroy must be obvious if you know he spent the night," Ann said.

"Un-huh."

"Jack DeRosa is my client."

"Un-huh."

"That they are both connected in some way to Nathan Smith is a coincidence."

"Un-huh."

"You don't believe in coincidence?"

"It doesn't get me anywhere," I said.

She nodded. I noticed her second drink was not going down nearly as quick as her first.

"And where are you trying to get?" she said.

"How come you represent Jack DeRosa?" I said.

"He needed a lawyer."

"And you were hanging around the public defender's office smiling hopefully?" I said.

"Every lawyer has a responsibility to the law," she said.

"So how'd DeRosa happen to hire you?" I said. "You bill more per hour than DeRosa's life is worth."

"Arrangements with clients are confidential."

"How about Conroy? What can you tell me about him?"

She smiled. "Relationships with friends are confidential."

"If there's something, Ms. Kiley, I'm going to find it."

"You don't frighten me, Mr. Spenser."

"Why not?"

"Mr. Spenser," she said, "you are a little man in a big arena. You simply don't matter."

"What about my nice personality?" I said.

"It doesn't interest me," Ann Kiley said. "Neither do you. Go away."

That seemed to sort of cover it. I put my drink down carefully on its coaster, got my hat and coat from the front hall closet, and left. Ann Kiley didn't see me to the door.

CHAPTER THIRTY-SIX

Belson called me at home, early. It was still a half hour before sunrise and the morning was still gray outside my bedroom window.

"I'm at a crime scene in your neighborhood," Belson said. "Wanna stop by?"

"Because you've missed me and you want to see me?" I said.

"Corner of Berkeley and Commonwealth," Belson said. "I'll look for you."

I walked over. There were the usual too many cop cars, lights still flashing. Two technicians were loading a body bag into the coroner's van. Belson in a light raincoat and a gray scally cap was leaning against his unmarked car, talking to one of the uniform guys. As I walked over, the uniform left.

"Hit and run," Belson said as I stopped beside him. "Vic's name is Brinkman Tyler."

"I know him," I said.

"Yeah. He had your card in his wallet."

"Just mine?"

"Hell no, he must have kept every card he ever got."

"But you called me," I said.

"I've missed you," Belson said. "And I wanted to see you."

"What happened?" I said.

"Near as we can figure, Brinkman was out jogging on the mall toward Arlington Street. He started across Berkeley Street and the car nailed him."

"Find the car?"

"Not yet. But it should have some damage on the front."

"Hit him at high speed," I said.

"Body looked it," Belson said. "ME's guys say so."

"What other cards he have in his wallet?" I said.

Belson took out a notebook and opened it.

"Well," he said. "He didn't have the Pope's card. Or Puff Daddy's."

"Can I look?"

Belson handed me the notebook.

"Absolutely not," Belson said. "This is a confidential police investigation."

I read the list of names and businesses that Belson had copied off the business cards of the late Brink. I recognized maybe a dozen names, but none that meant anything to my case. I gave Belson back his notebook.

"He was Nathan Smith's broker," I said. "Mary Smith said he managed her finances."

"So you went and talked with him."

"Yep. That's how he got my card."

"And?"

"And Brink told me nothing, even though I asked really nice, and after I left his office, two guys assaulted me in the parking garage."

"An assault you reported immediately to the proper authority," Belson said.

"I told Susan," I said.

Belson nodded. "These guys say why they were assaulting you?"

"They wanted to know what I'd talked with Brink about."

"And you, being you, probably didn't tell them."

"Client confidentiality is job one," I said.

"Sure," Belson said. "You know who these guys were?"

"They'd been following me around since I took the case."

"And you didn't mention it," Belson said.

"I wanted to see what got their attention."

Belson nodded. "Maybe this guy got their attention."

"Maybe."

"And maybe he'd be alive now if you'd felt like telling us about him."

"Maybe," I said. "Or maybe it's just an accident and the driver panicked and left the scene."

"Didn't some broad you talked to commit suicide?"

"That's what you guys are calling it," I said.

"And didn't somebody try to hit you the other night over on A Street?"

"Yep."

"And you talk to this guy and he's accidentally run down at five in the morning, at the intersection of two empty streets?"

"Seems to be the case," I said.

"That bother you?" Belson said.

"All of it bothers me," I said.

"Maybe this wasn't an accident," Belson said.

"And maybe Amy Peters wasn't a suicide," I said.

"And maybe you told us a little more about what you're doing, some of these people might not be dead."

"I don't know what I'm doing, Frank. If I did I'd tell you in a heartbeat."

"I owe you, Spenser," Belson said. "But I don't owe you everything there is all the time. You know something about a murder, you tell me."

"You don't owe me a thing, Frank. I know anything, you'll be my first phone call."

The uniform that Belson had been talking to when I arrived came back to Belson.

"Found the car, Frank. On Charles Street, a block up from the circle. Black Chrysler. Front end buckled. Phony plates."

Belson looked at me. "Wasn't there a black Chrysler involved in your shooting in Southie?"

"Yes."

"Had phony plates, as I recall."

"I believe so," I said. "I put a couple bullets through the roof."

Belson looked at the uniform.

"Got that, Pat?" he said.

"I got it, Frank."

"Go down there yourself," Belson said. "I want Crime Scene all over that car."

"Okay, Frank."

Belson turned to me as the uniform walked toward his car.

"This thing reeks," he said.

"It does."

"I got things to do here. Come see me tomorrow."

I nodded.

"And think about whether this guy might be alive if you'd told us what you know."

"I do what I can, Frank."

Belson looked at me for a time and nodded slowly.

"Yeah," he said. "I know you do."

CHAPTER THIRTY-SEVEN

Mary Smith wouldn't talk to me without Rita there, and apparently she wouldn't talk with Rita unless Larson Graff was present. We met for lunch at Aujourd'hui in the Four Seasons Hotel. It felt like a double date.

Most of the people and all of the men watched Rita walk in. She was dressed for success in a dark green suit with a short skirt and a V-necked jacket. Her smooth tan looked healthy even though it wasn't, and her thick red hair was in perfect shape. Susan had told me that red-haired women needed to make up with particular care, and Rita appeared to have done it just right.

In her beige pantsuit and careful blond hair, Mary looked a little pallid next to Rita. Larson looked like Larson and I remained dashing and ineffable. Mary had a champagne cocktail. The rest of us sipped Perrier.

"Why didn't you authorize me to see your husband's investment statements?" I said to Mary.

"Whaat?"

"Brink Tyler called you from his office and asked you if you'd authorize him to show me your husband's investment statements," I said.

"He did?"

I nodded.

"I don't remember that."

"Last week," I said. "About three-thirty in the afternoon, on a Tuesday."

"I get so many calls," Mary said.

Rita was sitting to my right at the table. She was sort of sideways to the table, half facing toward me with her legs crossed. She smiled when I looked at her and carefully hitched her skirt hem up another inch on her thigh.

"I was there when he called you," I said.

"I don't remember," she said.

I looked at Rita again.

"Mary," Rita said, "we're all on the same side here. If you can help him, you should."

"Oh, Rita, I know. I know that. I really, really do. But you wouldn't want me to lie about something. I absolutely can't remember Brink Tyler calling me up last Tuesday."

"When's the last time you talked with him?" I said.

Mary had some champagne cocktail to help her think. Any help was welcome.

"I can't really recall. Larson? Do you recall when I talked with Brink last?"

"I believe you and he spoke shortly after Nathan's death. He was handling the estate."

"Yes. That's right. Brink came over. He was so kind. He said he'd take care of everything."

"The broker's handling the estate?" I said.

"He's an attorney as well," Rita said.

"Renaissance man," I said. "Aren't you ashamed, Rita, just doing *law* law?"

"And that badly," Rita said.

"And how is your estate?"

Mary looked a little vague. "Fine."

She looked at Rita.

"Estate's in a kind of legal limbo," Rita said. "Until the cause of death gets clarified a little."

"Do you know how much you've inherited?" I said.

Mary shook her head. "Nathan always said we didn't talk about our money. That it wasn't dignified."

"It might be dignified to know how much you had," I said.

She looked helplessly at Larson Graff.

"Mary, I'm sorry. I'm in no position to know your finances."

"Well," Mary said. "Certainly your bill is always paid on time, Larson."

"Oh yes. It certainly is," Larson said.

The waitress brought lunch, which consisted of three salads and a sandwich. I got the sandwich.

"So, just so I understand," I said to Mary. "You don't know what your financial situation is, or you know, and feel it's undignified to say?"

Mary looked down at her salad. She speared a small slice of avocado and put it delicately in her mouth and chewed it more vigorously, I thought, than it required. When she had swallowed it, she took another sip of her champagne cocktail. Mary was dumb. But she moved very slowly. She looked at me and laughed as if she might be embarrassed.

"I don't really know, Mr. Spenser."

"Do you object if I find out?" I said.

"Well, I really."

She looked at Larson. Larson wasn't helpful. She looked at Rita. Rita nodded firmly.

"Well, I really think it's kind of, I don't want to be offensive, but I really think it's kind of nosy."

"God forbid," I said.

Rita smiled.

"You never got a call from Brink Tyler last Tuesday asking if Spenser could look at the investment statements?"

"Oh, Rita, I'm just so sure he didn't."

Rita looked at me. I looked at Rita.

"So who'd he call?" Rita said.

CHAPTER THIRTY-EIGHT

Hawk was in my office when I returned. He was sitting in my chair with his feet up on my desk, reading Simon Schama's *History of Britain*.

"You interested in British history?" I said when I came in.

"Naw. Read this dude's book on Rembrandt. I like him."

"Lot of big words," I said.

"Thought you could help me."

"White man's burden," I said. "Gimme my chair."

Hawk grinned and dog-eared his page and closed the book and got up and came around and plonked in a client chair. I sat at my desk.

"There," I said. "You looking for a place to sleep?"

"Nope. Since I ain't following anybody for you at the moment,

170

and since somebody tried to shoot your ass the other night, I thought maybe I should hang around with you, case somebody try again."

"Plus," I said, "you could learn a lot."

"Be a privilege," Hawk said. "Whyn't you bring me up to date on what you doing, so I'll know who to shoot."

I did. Hawk listened without expression, his face the pleasantly impenetrable blank it always was.

"You got more information than you can handle," Hawk said when I got through.

"I do," I said.

" 'Course it easy for you to have too much information."

"How about yourself," I said. "You make anything out of it?"

Hawk grinned at me. "I'm just a simple thug," he said. "I ain't supposed to make nothing out of it."

"That may be true of me," I said.

"Simple thug?"

"Yeah."

"Thing is, all of the stuff you know doesn't add up to who done what."

"That is the thing," I said.

"You tell Mary her husband was gay?"

"No."

"Rita gonna find out about Smith's finances for you?"

"Yes."

"When she do you'll have more information."

"And I still won't know anything."

"Be used to that," Hawk said. "You think Mary lying, or you think the Brinkster call himself?"

"If he did," I said, "it would be sort of a stopgap. He had to know I'd ask her myself pretty soon."

"Maybe he figure you ain't around, pretty soon."

"Because he knew somebody would hit me," I said.

Hawk nodded. "Or maybe he did call her," he said. "And she lying when she say he didn't."

"Which might mean the same thing," I said. "Except she's so goddamned dumb."

"Dumb enough to think you wouldn't check on her?"

"She gets by with dumb," I said. "She uses it. She may even rely on it."

"There got to be some money in here someplace," Hawk said.

"See, that's just the reason you're a hooligan and I'm a detective," I said. "You jump to conclusions. I search for clues."

"Here's a clue," Hawk said. "A banker, a financial guy, a real estate developer, and a lawyer. All connected in some way to a homicide."

"Gee, you think there's money involved?"

"How I know. You the detective. I is just a hoo-li-gan."

"At least we're clear on that," I said. "Maybe we should revisit Jack DeRosa."

"The jailbird? Why him?"

"Can't think of anybody else?" I said.

Hawk grinned.

" 'Least he fit on the list," Hawk said. "Right after lawyer."

THIRTY-NINE

I called Frank Belson and asked him if we could arrange to talk with DeRosa again. He called me back in an hour.

"DeRosa's been out of jail for a week," he said. "Eyewitness couldn't pick him out of a lineup."

"Charges dropped?"

"Yep."

"Got an address for him?"

"Got the one he had when they busted him," Frank said, and gave me the name of a street off Andrews Square.

In half an hour Hawk and I were crossing the bridge on Southampton Street. We were in Hawk's Jaguar. Hawk parked it behind a place that sold orthotics, where it was about as incon-spicuous in South Boston as Hawk was. We walked across the street to a brick duplex, which had a tiny front yard that had been carpeted with gray stone and surrounded by a chain-link fence. The downstairs windows were grated. There was a peephole in the front door.

"DeRosa don't seem interested in botany," Hawk said.

"He's probably just a renter," I said.

"Landlord's a geologist?" Hawk said.

Above the doorbell button beside the right-hand door was a small hand-lettered card that said *DeRosa/McDermott*. I rang. No one answered. I rang again. Same thing. Hawk reached over and rang the doorbell on the left-hand door. Nobody answered. I looked through the peephole the wrong way, like I always did, and I found that I couldn't see anything in that direction. Like I always did. I tried the door. It was locked. Hawk nodded and walked back across the street to the Jaguar and opened the trunk, took out a big red gym bag, and came back across the street with it. He set it down on the steps and took out a flat bar and handed it to me.

"Why do you have one if you can't use it?" I said.

"I use it when I haven't got an Irish-American laborer handy."

I took the flat bar and got it wedged in against the doorjamb where the lock tongue would be and heaved and there was some doorjamb splintering and then the bolt tore loose and the door popped free. I put the flat bar back in the red gym bag and handed it to Hawk.

"Tote that bale," I said.

He took it back to the Jaguar. No one in the neighborhood seemed interested that I had just performed the B part of a B & E.

I pushed the door open. The lock I had jimmied was the kind that locked behind you when you went out. The house was silent. And hot. And stuffy. Lights were on in the hallway. I smelled a bad smell. Hawk came in behind me from his bale-toting chores. I could hear him breathe in.

"Whoops," Hawk said.

I nodded and, breathing through my mouth, started through the front hall toward what was probably the living room. I knew what I would find. Hawk walked beside me. Inside the living room archway we both stopped.

"Jesus," I said.

"Un-huh," Hawk said.

The distorted remains of a man and woman lay together on the floor, their bodies disfigured by the slow flame of decay. The woman sprawled diagonally across the man. Someone had shot them many times, probably with an automatic weapon, maybe more than one. They had, in the process, chopped the room up pretty good. Pieces of chair backs, scraps of upholstery, bits of lamp shade, shards of glass, and fragments of plastic, and plaster, and human tissue clung to the walls. The blood covered the floor, black by now, and hardened like a vast scab. Insects had found them both. The room was very hot and flies buzzed thickly in the stinking air.

I had seen it before, but I never liked it. And this was worse than most. Except that I could hear him breathing through his mouth, Hawk showed no sign that it bothered him. For all that showed on his face, he could have been looking at a lawn tractor.

"DeRosa?" he said.

"I assume so," I said. "And maybe McDermott as well."

Hawk walked over to the corpses and looked down at them.

"Hard to be sure," Hawk said. "McDermott the girlfriend?"

"I dunno. It's the other name on the doorbell."

"People dying just after you talk to them or just before," Hawk said. "Somebody think you closing in?"

"I guess so," I said. "Wish I had their confidence."

"We pretty clear on what happened to these folks," Hawk said. "You think Amy Peters a suicide?"

"No."

"You believe Brink Tyler an accident victim?"

"No."

Hawk was still staring down at the bodies. He shook his head a little to dispel a fly.

"They shot these people to pieces," Hawk said. "I bet they got fifteen, twenty rounds apiece in them."

"Had to make some noise," I said.

"Anybody heard it, they ignored it," Hawk said. "These people been here awhile."

I looked around the living room. The windows were shut and locked. There was a big air-conditioning unit in a side window. I looked at it. It was turned off.

"When's the last time it was cool?" I said.

Hawk shrugged.

"Don't do weather," he said.

We went through the house, living room and kitchen on the first floor. Two bedrooms and a bath on the second. The smell thickened the air in every room. All the windows were closed and locked. The air conditioner in the second-floor bedroom was shut off, too. The back door was locked. In the drawer of the front hall table we found a 9mm Colt, with a round jacked up into the chamber.

"Man locked everything," Hawk said. "Yep. No windows open, even if it be cool when he shut off the AC, most people like a little ventilation in the summer."

"It's not a bad neighborhood," I said. "But he was being pretty careful. Gun in the front hall. Round in the chamber."

Hawk nodded. "He knew them," Hawk said.

"Seems like it," I said.

"He would have looked through the peephole," I said. "And he would have unlocked the door when he saw them. The hall gun is still in the drawer. He wasn't afraid of them."

"And he should have been," Hawk said. "You figure the broad got shot because she was here?"

"Could be. Or it could be she was part of the whole deal. Whatever the whole deal was. Or it could be they wanted to kill her, and he had the misfortune to be on hand."

"Going to call the cops?" Hawk said.

"Guess we got to."

"We could just close the door and walk away."

"Your fingerprints in the system?" I said.

" 'Course," Hawk said.

"Mine too."

"So give them a call," Hawk said.

FORTY

"We'll let the B and E slide," Quirk said. "But corpses keep show-ing up in your area, we might cite you for littering."

We were outside, away from the smell, leaning on the fender of Quirk's car. It was about six hours since we'd found the bodies. The prowl car guys had arrived first and questioned us and told us to stick around. Some District 6 detectives came and asked us ques-tions and told us to stick around. Crime scene people asked us questions and told us the detectives wanted us to stick around. Belson showed up after a while and asked us questions and told us to stick around and wait for Quirk. An hour and a half ago Quirk had ambled in and told us to stick around until he was through.

"Anyone know the identity of the woman?" I said.

"Yeah, we talked with some neighbors. Name was Margaret Mc-

Dermott. She was DeRosa's girlfriend. Live-in. Been with him six, eight years," Quirk said.

He was looking at Hawk. Hawk smiled at him.

"You bother me," Quirk said. "I know you wouldn't have aced these two people, then come back a week later and called us."

Hawk smiled some more.

"And I know that when you're with Snoop Doggy Dogg here, you may not be on the up-and-up, but you're probably not illegal."

Hawk's smile seemed almost sweet as he listened to Quirk.

"On the other hand," Quirk said, "I hate to come upon a double homicide and find you lingering about and give you a bye."

I said, "I'm pretty sure he didn't do it, Captain."

"I'm pretty sure he didn't, too," Quirk said. "But not because you say so."

"My word is my bond," I said.

"I don't know what the connection is between you two clowns, but I know you'd cover for him."

"White guilt," I said. "My ancestors might have owned slaves."

"Yo' ancestors being bog-trotting paddies didn't have the money to own no slaves," Hawk said.

I looked at him sadly. "You wouldn't understand," I said. "It's a white thing."

"Isn't this fun," Quirk said. "Lemme get the other cops over here, give them a chance to listen."

I said, "We're just working on our material, Captain."

"And it's really enjoyable," Quirk said. "Oddly enough there's no warrants out on Hawk."

"You sure?" Hawk said.

"I had it checked."

"Embarrassing," Hawk said.

"You got anything you can tell me about this thing?" Quirk said.

"Same as I tole the other six cops," Hawk said. "I just along try to keep him from hurting himself."

"Okay, you can drift," Quirk said. "Spenser, I'll talk a little more with you."

Hawk nodded his head once, slightly, and walked away.

"I talked to the same six cops he did," I said.

"You used to be a cop," Quirk said. "You know how we do this." I nodded.

"I don't know much more than I did after I shot the guy in Southie," I said.

"You didn't know much before you shot that guy in Southie. Name was Kevin McGonigle. Twenty-three, two priors for strong-arm."

"Good to start young," I said.

"And finish that way," Quirk said.

I shrugged. "Him or me," I said.

"I know. Tell me what you know," Quirk said.

We were both leaning against Quirk's car. Quirk's arms were folded across his chest, and he was motionless except for the fact that the fingers on his thick right hand tapped gently on his left arm.

"Okay," I said. "It's a mishmash, but here it is, all of it."

I told him everything in sequence from the time Rita had

called me about Mary Smith until Hawk and I had come to visit DeRosa.

"You got a theory?" Quirk said.

"No."

"If you count Nathan Smith," Quirk said, "and I do, there's him, the broad from the bank . . ."

"Amy Peters," I said.

". . . Tyler, DeRosa, the girlfriend, Kevin McGonigle."

"Six," I said.

"And all connected to you, one way or another."

"Charisma," I said.

"Six murders," Quirk said. "And somebody threatens to beat you up and somebody hires McGonigle to clip you, and you got no theory?"

"There's something being covered up," I said. "And it's connected to Nathan Smith."

"Holy mackerel," Quirk said.

"You asked."

Quirk nodded. We watched the body bags load into the ME's van.

"We find out anything, we'll tell each other," I said.

"I known you a long time," Quirk said.

I didn't comment. Quirk wasn't really talking to me anyway. A couple of uniforms moved the small crowd out of the way as the ME's van pushed slowly among them, hauling away the unpleasant remains of DeRosa and his girlfriend.

"And you are a stubborn bastard, and you don't much give a fuck about how things are supposed to go."

Quirk was still looking at the van. A uniform stopped traffic. The van turned left onto Southampton Street and moved slowly over the bridge.

"And you're not as smart as you think you are, and nowhere near as funny," Quirk said, still watching the van as it disappeared toward downtown. "But you're on the right side of the fence."

"How do you know it's the right side?" I said.

"Same side I'm on," Quirk said.

FORTY-ONE

We were in Hawk's car. It was 10:15 on a bright summer morning when we pulled into the parking lot at Soldiers Field Development Limited. We had no trouble parking. The lot was empty. The front door of the building was locked. There was no sign of movement or light inside.

"B and E?" Hawk said.

"Might as well," I said. "Practice makes perfect."

Hawk handed me the flat bar, and in we went. There was no air-conditioning. The building was hot. The furniture was still in place. But no one was using it. We walked down the corridor to the back office where Felton Shawcross had sat. The corridor was dim. There were no lights on. There was a bank of file cabinets across the right wall of Shawcross's office. I opened a drawer. It was empty. I opened them all. They were empty. Hawk looked in Shawcross's desk. It was empty. He picked up the phone.

"Dial tone," he said.

I tried a light switch. The lights went on.

"Didn't bother to cancel anything," I said.

We went methodically down the row of offices that lined each side of the long corridor. All of them were empty. All of the files were empty. The only things in the desk drawers were a few Bic pens, some blank paper, some rubber bands, paper clips, staples, and pads of yellow stick 'em paper to draw smiley faces on.

"Didn't leave no paper trail," Hawk said. "Maybe they skipping out on the utility bills."

"Probably it," I said.

We had worked our way down the corridor and were standing in the reception area. There was no place else to look.

"On the wall in the men's room it say for a good time call 555-1212," Hawk said.

"Probably a clue," I said.

A mailman in blue shorts came in carrying a packet of mail held together by a wide rubber band. He looked around.

"You guys moving out?" he said.

"Just rehabbing," I said. "Closed for a couple of weeks."

"You oughta notify us, fill out a form, have us hold your mail until you're back in business."

"What a very good idea," I said. "My man here will be down to the post office later today to fill out the documents."

"It's just a form," the mailman said. "What do I do with this mail?"

"I'll take it," I said.

He handed me the mail and left.

"*My man* be down to the post office?" Hawk said.

"I'm cleaning up my act," I said. "There was a time I would have said *my boy*."

"I love a liberal," Hawk said.

I took the mail over to the reception desk and went though it with Hawk looking over my shoulder. We went through it twice. Each of us. To make sure we hadn't missed anything. There was nothing to miss. People like this didn't do business by mail. When we were through I left the mail in a neat pile on the reception desk.

"The more we look, the more there's nothing there," Hawk said.

I sat back in the receptionist chair and leaned back against the spring.

"We keep getting there just afterwards," I said.

"Getting where?" Hawk said.

"I don't know," I said.

"Least they didn't shoot nobody and leave them for us."

"No."

"Maybe there ain't no one left to shoot," Hawk said.

I was rocked back, looking at the Celotex ceiling tiles, my hands laced over my chest.

"Ann Kiley," I said.

"Ann Kiley?"

"She was DeRosa's lawyer."

"So."

"She's got no business representing a stiff like DeRosa."

"Nice choice of words," Hawk said.

I shrugged.

"If DeRosa was killed so we wouldn't find out anything from him, what are the chances that his lawyer would know what that is?"

"The chances are good," Hawk said. "And even if they aren't, the people who killed DeRosa might think they were."

I came forward in the spring-back chair, letting my feet hit the ground. I pointed my finger at Hawk and dropped my thumb like the hammer on a gun.

"Let's go see her," I said. "Right now."

"So we won't be afterwards again?"

"So that," I said.

CHAPTER

FORTY-TWO

Ann Kiley had the second biggest corner office on the twenty-fifth floor of a high-rise on Broad Street. Her father had the biggest, the one that looked out to sea. Ann had what the real estate ads would call cityscape views.

I introduced Hawk when we came in, and they eyed each other, evaluating potential.

"So where's Harbaugh's office?" I said when we were seated.

Ann pointed toward the ceiling.

"Big firm in the sky," she said.

"So this place is really Kiley and Kiley."

"Yes. But the name was familiar, so we decided to leave it."

I could tell, as she spoke, that she was aware of Hawk. Silent, as he often was, there was still a lot of Hawk.

"Did you know that Jack DeRosa was murdered?" I said.

"Yes."

"What do you think?"

"About DeRosa's death?"

"Yes."

"No one should be murdered," she said.

"Are you in danger?"

Hawk stood and walked to the window and looked out.

"Danger? Why would I be in danger?"

"Because I'm pretty sure DeRosa was killed to shut him up, and if he talked with you, they might feel they had to shut you up, too."

"That's absurd," Ann Kiley said. "I was Jack's attorney. Nothing more."

I looked at Hawk. She saw me look and turned and looked at him, too. Hawk smiled.

"You fuck around with this," Hawk said, "and they gonna kill you, too."

She was tough, but it rocked her. Hawk saying it made it some-how more forceful. I have often wondered how he got that effect, and have finally concluded that it is because he doesn't care. Doesn't care if she believes him. Doesn't care if they kill her, too. She was too contained to show it much, but there was a faint look of strain around her eyes and in the way her mouth compressed.

"I have no idea," she said, "what either of you is talking about."

There was a short knock on her office door, and it opened im-mediately and Bobby Kiley walked in. He closed the door behind him.

"I'd like to sit in," he said to his daughter.

"I don't think I need any help," Ann Kiley said.

"I'll sit in anyway," Kiley said. "How are you, Spenser?"

"Fine, Bobby. Nice to see you."

He walked over to Hawk and put out a hand.

"Bobby Kiley," he said.

"Hawk."

Kiley nodded and walked back to sit in a chair beside me. He was a handsome guy with white hair and one of those slightly hollow-cheeked Irish faces.

"What's up?" he said.

"Bobby," Ann said, "why are you here?"

"I know this guy." He nodded at me. "I know somebody killed a guy we represent."

"I can handle this myself," Ann said.

Kiley shrugged and stayed where he was.

"You know Nathan Smith?" I said.

"Know of him," Kiley said. "Know he was murdered."

"I was hired by Cone Oakes to investigate his death," I said.

Kiley nodded. Ann Kiley sat perfectly still. She looked like she was insulted by her father's intervention. But she also didn't look strained around the mouth and eyes anymore.

"Rita," Kiley said.

"Yep."

"Hell of a lawyer," Kiley said.

"And when I started looking into the matter," I said, "people started to die. A woman at Smith's bank committed suicide. Smith's broker was killed in a hit-and-run. A kid named Kevin McGonigle tried to kill me."

"Heard about that," Kiley said. "You got him first."

"Then Jack DeRosa got shot and his girlfriend with him."

"Our client," Kiley said.

"Ann represented him."

"And?"

"And that's too many people dying in the same case."

"I agree," Kiley said. "So?"

"So Smith is on the board of a company named Soldiers Field Development, which had some of its employees following me after I started the case. We talked with them, and this morning we went out to talk with them again. They had packed up and left."

"Suspicious," Kiley said.

"There's a guy who came in as Smith's partner at the bank not too long before Smith was shot. Guy named Marvin Conroy."

Kiley frowned a little. As if the name meant something.

"Marvin Conroy is an acquaintance of your daughter's."

Kiley glanced neutrally at Ann. "Yeah?"

"And Ann was representing DeRosa when he told us that Mary Smith hired him to kill her husband."

"This is all very interesting," Kiley said. "But I was hoping you might sort of get around to why you are here talking to my daughter."

"This is the preeminent criminal law practice in the city. Maybe on the East Coast. What the hell are you doing with Jack DeRosa?"

"He was Ann's client," Kiley said. "Ask her."

"That's where we were when you came in," I said.

Kiley smiled and didn't say anything.

"So," I said to Ann, "how'd you come to represent DeRosa?"

"I decline to discuss my clients with you," she said.

"Tell me," Kiley said.

"Bobby," his daughter said, "I am not going to talk about this with these men."

"I want to know, Ann."

Father and daughter stared at each other. I stayed quiet. Hawk leaned placidly against the wall, looking at the view. Then Kiley shifted his gaze to me.

"There any connection between this guy Marvin Conroy and DeRosa?"

"Conroy was in the bank with Smith," I said. "DeRosa was asked to kill Smith."

"That's hardly a connection," Kiley said.

"Yet," I said.

Kiley shifted his glance to Hawk. "I been in the criminal defense business for a long time," Kiley said. "I know what he does."

"And well," I said.

"He watching your back?"

"Yes."

"So this is serious business," Kiley said, probably to himself more than to me. He pointed his chin at Ann Kiley. "You think she's in danger?"

Ann said, "I'm not a she. My name is Ann."

I nodded. "I think Ann's in danger," I said.

Kiley said, "What do you think, Ann?"

"I think it's preposterous," she said.

"No," Kiley said. "I know this guy. He thinks you're in danger, we need to take it seriously."

"For God's sake, Bobby—"

"And cut the Bobby shit, for the moment. It's fine while we're colleagues, but I'm also your father, and I want to know what the fuck is going on. How come we represented Jack DeRosa?"

Ann Kiley's face got very tight, and colorless. Her jaw clamped, but do what she would, she couldn't stop it. She began to cry. She stood and walked to the window and stood beside Hawk and looked out. Her shoulders shook, though not very much. In the quiet room we could hear the stifled sound of her fight for control. Bobby Kiley didn't move. Hawk looked at me. I looked at Hawk. We decided that quiet was the way to go.

After a time Ann turned from the window. She had stopped crying, but her eyes were red and her face was stiff. She leaned her hips against the window ledge and folded her arms and looked straight at her father.

"I'm having an affair with Marvin Conroy," she said.

Kiley nodded. Ann Kiley took in a long slow breath with a hint of vibrato.

"It's a serious affair," she said.

Kiley nodded again. Ann tightened her folded arms as if she were hugging herself in a cold place.

"He asked me to help him," she said. "He was in trouble."

Nobody said anything. The phone rang on Ann Kiley's desk. Bobby Kiley picked it up and said, "No calls," and hung up.

"He asked me if I could find him someone to pretend something. He said I was a criminal lawyer, and I should be able to find someone."

"And you found DeRosa," Bobby Kiley said.

"Yes."

"How?"

"I was doing my annual pro bono, for the public defender's office, as required by the firm, and I drew DeRosa, some sort of auto theft, I believe."

"So when Conroy wanted a mug you remembered DeRosa."

Kiley appeared calm. He seemed entirely focused on the questions he was asking and the answers he was getting.

"And Marvin asked me to be DeRosa's lawyer, this time, too, to see that he stayed on message."

"The message being?"

"That Mary Smith had approached him to kill her husband."

"Which was not true," Kiley said.

"No. I don't believe it was."

Kiley sat back in his chair. Hawk and I remained where we were. Ann Kiley said, "Daddy."

Kiley stood and went to her and opened his arms and she fell against him and began to cry. As he hugged her, he looked at me.

"We can talk later," he said.

"You will need security for her," I said.

"I know," Kiley said. "I can arrange that."

"There's more I need to know," I said.

"She's got nothing else to say," Kiley said.

"I think she does," I said.

"Doesn't matter what you think," Kiley said.

CHAPTER FORTY-THREE

It was Sunday. I was drinking coffee with my right hand and driving with my left. Pearl was asleep in the backseat, and Susan was beside me drinking coffee from a big paper cup which she held in both hands. We were on the road to Newburyport, and we had chosen to take the old Route 1, through the slow rural landscape north of Boston.

"How's your lawsuit?" I said.

"I think the insurance company plans to settle," Susan said.

"Thus leaving you neither vindicated nor convicted."

"But they'll probably cancel afterwards," she said.

"Insurance companies are fun," I said. "Aren't they."

Susan nodded. She dipped into her coffee, her big eyes gazing at the road across the top of the cup.

"And the boy is still dead," she said.

"And it's still not your fault," I said.

She was quiet, her face still half hidden by the coffee. In the backseat Pearl snored occasionally, the way she had begun to do as she got older.

"Fault has little to do with sadness," Susan said. "One of the things that helps kids get through the difficulty of being a gay adolescent is to have someone. I don't mean a shrink. But a friend, a lover, someone. But the thing they need help with prevents them from getting it."

"Because they're too conflicted about being homosexual," I said.

"I hate that word," Susan said into her cup.

"Homosexual?"

"Yes."

"Too clinical?"

"Makes me think of grim men in lab coats," Susan said. "Studying a pathology."

I had nothing to say about that, and decided in this case to try saying nothing. Susan drank her coffee. I drank mine.

"Where's Hawk?" Susan said.

"I thought we'd have Sunday alone together."

"Except for the baby."

"Except for her."

"Is it safe?"

"Even without Hawk," I said, "I am not an amateur."

"True," Susan said. "Have you ever considered that your person might have been suicidal?"

"Nathan Smith?"

"Yes. A closeted gay man. Trying to pretend."

"There was no gun," I said.

"Too bad, he so fit the profile. A life spent in deception, finally too much."

I shrugged.

"How are you with this kid's death?" I said.

"I've gone over every therapy session ten times."

"You remember them all?"

"Yes."

"And?"

"And I did what there was to do," Susan said.

"And better than most people could have," I said.

"How do you know," Susan said. "You've never been in therapy with me."

I smiled.

"Why, this is therapy," I said. "Nor am I out of it."

"Hamlet?" Susan said.

"Mephistopheles," I said.

"Who?"

"Marlowe," I said. *"Doctor Faustus."*

"Smarty-pants."

"So how come I can't figure out what's going on with the Nathan Smith thing?"

"I'll bet you could if Christopher Marlowe did it."

"A slam dunk," I said.

"Have you thought about what kind of woman marries a gay man?" Susan said.

"Yes."

"Do you have a conclusion?"

"No. I can't figure her out."

"Maybe you need to," Susan said. "Maybe you need to find out more about Mr. Smith's life as a gay man. Maybe you need to find out why Mrs. Smith married him."

"A tip?" I said. "A crime-stopper tip?"

"Two tips," Susan said. "I have a Ph.D. from Harvard."

"A hotbed of crime-stopping," I said.

"A hotbed," Susan said.

We drove on to Newburyport. Susan shopped. Pearl and I stood outside each shop, and waited. Pearl slept in the car while we ate lunch at the Black Cow. Susan and Pearl and I went for a walk on the beach at Plum Island. None of us talked about business for the rest of the day.

CHAPTER

FORTY-FOUR

I went over to Pequod Bank on Monday morning to talk with Marvin Conroy. He wasn't there. I said I would wait. They were cool with it. I sat in a chair and watched people discuss checking accounts and loans for three hours. At noon I asked if there was a number for Conroy. There was. But they couldn't give me his home phone number.

"Could you call him for me?" I said.

The acting second assistant junior auxiliary vice president who was working with me looked startled.

"Me? Call him at home?"

"You. Yes."

"Is it, ah, an emergency?" she said.

"Life and death," I said.

"Not really?" she said.

"Really," I said.

She hesitated. I fixed her with my gleaming blue stare. She shrugged and opened her Rolodex and picked up the phone. She gave her hair a little toss to get the phone in under it, and dialed a number. I waited. She was wearing one of those thin, loose-fitting ankle-length flowered dresses that women sometimes wore in Cambridge, I assumed in tribute to a long-gone hippie past. Hers was especially sporty, tan with brown flowers. Whether there was any kind of worthwhile body going on underneath there was difficult to say, but I was ready to give her the benefit of the doubt.

She hung up the phone.

"I'm sorry," she said. "There's no answer. Would you like to leave a message for him?"

"You have an address for him?" I said.

"Certainly not," she said.

I glanced at her Rolodex and she grabbed it and clutched it to her as if she were protecting its virtue. I smiled at her.

"You've been more than kind," I said.

Back in my car I called Bobby Kiley's office. Argued with the switchboard operator, and the receptionist, and Kiley's secretary until I got through.

"It would be easier calling the Pope," I said, when he was on the phone.

"But less useful," Kiley said. "What do you want?"

"How's Ann?"

"She's lousy."

"I need to know Marvin Conroy's address," I said.

"I'll call you back," Kiley said.

I gave him my car phone number, which I could never remember and therefore had written on a piece of paper tucked over the sun visor. Then I sat and looked at life in East Cambridge for maybe ten minutes until Kiley called back.

Conroy lived in an apartment in the North End on Commercial Street across from the Coast Guard station and a little ways down the street from the old garage where the Brink's Robbery had taken place. I went up four cement steps and looked at the small sign that said NORTH CHURCH REALTY. LONG AND SHORT TERM RENTALS. I read the names on the mailboxes. Conroy was on the second floor. I rang. No luck. There were seven other names on the mailboxes. I rang all of them. Only one person, a woman, who sounded sleepy, answered through the speaker.

"Hi," I said. "I'm from the cable company. We need to check some terminals."

"Well, check them some other time, pal," the woman said. "I'm trying to take a freakin' nap."

The speaker went dead. Okay, if the terminals went bad it wasn't my fault. I leaned my fanny on the black iron porch rail and thought about it. As I was thinking a young man in a gray suit and big glasses came up the steps with his key out. I fumbled in my pockets.

"Oh God," I said. "I'm staying in 2B and I can't find my keys."

He smiled blankly and nodded and opened the door. I walked in right behind him. He disappeared into the elevator. I took the stairs. When I got to Conroy's place, I looked around in the small hallway. There was only one other apartment. I went to it and knocked on the door. No one answered. I went back to Conroy's door and kicked it in.

Inside was bedroom, sitting room, bath, kitchenette. It was charmless and impersonal. It showed little signs of occupancy. Cereal in the kitchen cabinet and half a loaf of bread, orange juice, and milk in the refrigerator. Two utility bills on the kitchen counter, both overdue. There were no clothes in the closet. No toiletries in the bath. A bath towel was crumpled on the floor. I picked it up. It was wrinkled, but no longer damp. There were no credit-card receipts, no answering machine with phone messages, no personal computer with e-mail messages. No clue at all about where Marvin Conroy had gone, or who he was.

CHAPTER

FORTY-FIVE

Maybe I should do what Susan said. I had rarely gotten in trouble doing that, and I had absolutely nowhere else to go. Susan had designated two areas of possible interest: Smith's sexual orientation, and his marriage. Since Larson Graff was an associate of Mrs. Smith, and pretty surely gay, I thought I might as well start with him. Given what I had, I might just as well have started with Liberace if he were still with us.

I took Larson to lunch at Grill 23. I was quite sure that Hawk would make Larson nervous, so he had a sandwich at the bar while Larson and I took a table against the Stuart Street wall.

"Things have changed," I said. "Several people have died. I'm going to need some truth here, Larson."

"I'll try to be forthcoming," he said.

"You'll need to be more so than you have been, I think."

I gave him the hard eye. Larson looked around the room.

"How did you come to know Mary Smith?" I said.

Larson ate a shrimp from his shrimp cocktail. He leaned back a moment to savor it, breathing in as if there were a bouquet to experience. I waited.

"Oh, I've known Mary forever," he said after he'd experienced his shrimp sufficiently.

"How long would that be," I said.

"Oh." He paused and sipped a small swallow of ice water and experienced that for a while. "Twenty years or so."

Since Mary was thirty that meant he'd known her as a child.

"You from Franklin?"

He didn't answer for a while. I waited. He couldn't stand the silence.

"Yes."

"You went to school with her?"

Again the pause. Again the wait. Again he capitulated.

"Grammar school, middle school, high school. Then I went on to college and she stayed in Franklin."

"Friends?"

"Oh yes. Tight. Buddies, really. Franklin wasn't the easiest place to grow up."

"There may not be any easy places," I said.

Larson carefully dabbed a little horseradish into his cocktail sauce. It bothered me that I hadn't come across his name.

"You know her other friends?" I said.

He smiled. Apparently he'd decided that frank disclosure might relieve tension.

"Sure," he said. "Roy, Pike, Tammy? Sure."

"How about Joey Bucci?"

Larson had ordered a glass of Chablis with his appetizer. He sipped a small sip of it, savored it self-consciously, and smiled at me.

"Why do you ask about Joey Bucci," he said.

"He was described as part of her group," I said. "Nobody mentioned you."

Larson had another shrimp. He looked thoughtful, but it might have been just his savoring look. He took in some air and let it out slowly.

Then he said, "I used to be Joey Bucci."

"You changed it," I said.

"I just didn't feel like a Joey Bucci," he said.

"You felt like a Larson Graff?"

He smiled. "In my business more Larson Graff and less Joey Bucci is a good thing," he said.

"Mary says you came to her through her husband."

"Only indirectly," Larson said. "He called and said Mary was looking for a public relations advisor and had asked him to call me. That's how I met him."

His shrimp cocktail was gone, leaving him more time to fully examine the remaining Chablis. It was his third.

"Through Mary?" I said.

My head was beginning to hurt.

"Yes."

"And you became friends independent of her?"

Larson smiled and tilted his head.

"We shared a common interest," he said.

"Young men?" I said.

"So. You know about Nathan?"

"I do."

"Poor old queen," Larson said. "Still deep in the closet in this day and age."

I nodded. He sipped his wine.

"Pathetic, really," Larson said.

"Mary says she met her husband through you."

He laughed. "That's Mary. She can't string five words together and make sense. She probably said it backwards from what she meant. I met Nathan through her."

I nodded. Old Mary. Dumb as a flounder. As opposed to me, the brainy crimebuster, who seemed to be losing brain cells every day he was on this case.

"If Nathan was gay, what do you suppose Mary did for a sex life?"

Larson laughed again. Having committed to the conversation, he seemed to have jumped in feet first.

"Some of us can go both ways," he said.

"Was Nathan one who could?"

"I don't think so," Graff said, a little singsong in his voice.

"So did Mary have any other possibilities for a sex life?"

"I hope so," Graff said.

"And if she did, would you have any candidates?"

"For fucking Mary?" Graff said. "Hard to narrow it down."

"She was promiscuous?"

"Oh," Graff said. "I don't know, really. I was being facetious."

"So when you're not being facetious," I said, "who would be a good candidate to, ah, help Mary out."

"I'd say," Larson almost giggled, "I'd say the fickle finger of suspicion points at Roy."

"Roy Levesque?" I said. "The former boyfriend?"

"Maybe once and future," Graff said.

"Any dates and places?" I said.

"No. Just a guess."

"Okay. You know anything about Smith's banking business?"

"No." Larson was working on his fourth glass of Chablis. "That's not the business he and I shared an interest in."

"Soldiers Field Development?" I said.

Graff shook his head.

I said, "Marvin Conroy? Felton Shawcross? Amy Peters? Jack DeRosa? Kevin McGonigle? Margaret McDermott?"

"I don't know any of those people," he said. "Conroy and Shawcross sound familiar. They might have been on Mary's invitation list. The others . . ." He shrugged, putting a lot into it.

"You have any idea," I said, "who killed Nathan Smith?"

"None," he said.

He stood. So I stood.

"Thanks for lunch," he said. "I really do have to get back to the office."

We shook hands. I watched him go. I thought of Jay Gatsby.

Somewhere back there, when he was a kid, Joey Bucci had invented just the kind of Larson Graff that a kid was likely to invent, and to that invention he was remaining faithful. I paid the check and when I left, Hawk eased off his bar stool and left with me. Which was comforting.

CHAPTER FORTY-SIX

Hawk and I reported in to Rita Fiore. Actually I was reporting to Rita, Hawk was along to help keep me from getting shot. Rita didn't mind. I knew she wouldn't. Hawk fascinated her. Among other things he was male, which gave him a running start on fascinating Rita.

"I think I want a raise," I said.

"And you don't want to take it out in trade?" Rita said.

"Perhaps my associate," I said.

Hawk smiled serenely.

"You think?" Rita said.

"One never knows," Hawk said. "Do one."

"Keep me in mind," Rita said, and to me, "Why do you need a raise?"

"Wear and tear on my brain," I said. "Every time I turn over a rock, there's three more rocks."

"I'll help you," Rita said. "Tell me about it."

She sat back in her big leather swivel chair and crossed her admirable legs and listened, while I told her about it. As far as I could tell, when she slipped into her professional mode, she banished all thoughts of sexual excess.

"Okay," she said when I finished. "Obviously there's something going on between Pequod Bank, and Soldiers Field Development, and Marvin Conroy."

"Yep."

"And there's probably something going on among Larson Graff, and Mary Smith, and the boyfriend, whatsisname."

"Roy Levesque."

"And maybe Ann Kiley is in there somewhere."

"Or maybe she's just Conroy's girlfriend and loved not wisely but too well," I said.

"Don't we all," Rita said. She looked at Hawk. "Except maybe you," she said.

Hawk smiled at her. Rita swung her crossed leg thoughtfully. She was wearing a red suit with a just barely street-legal skirt. The suit went surprisingly well with her red hair.

"You've got a bank and a development company in some sort of uncertain relationship," I said. "That raise any flags?"

Rita nodded. "I'll talk with Abner Grove," she said. "He's our tax and finance guy. See what he can find out."

"It may not help your client," I said.

"If I am going to put up the best defense I can, I need to know as much as I can. I'm not obliged to use it all. What you can do is come at this from the other end."

"Mary, Larson, and Roy," I said.

"Sounds like a singing group."

"Maybe it will be," I said.

"So you start from your end, and we'll start from ours, and maybe we'll meet in the middle."

"Or maybe we won't," I said.

"Coincidences do exist."

"They do," I said.

"You think they exist in this case?"

"No."

Rita eyed Hawk, who appeared to be thinking of faraway places. I knew he wasn't. Hawk always knew everything that was going on around him.

"What do you think about coincidence," Rita said to him.

"Hard to prepare for," Hawk said.

CHAPTER FORTY-SEVEN

Hawk and I drove down to Franklin in Hawk's Jaguar.

"Figure you show up in a decent ride," Hawk said, "they be impressed and tell you everything."

"You bet," I said. "That's how it usually works."

We found Roy Levesque at the lumberyard where he worked. He wore jeans and work boots and a plaid shirt that hung outside his pants.

"Whaddya want," Levesque said.

The yard was loud with the sound of a band saw, and busy with trucks loading lumber and Sheetrock.

"See the car I came in?" I said.

"I don't give a fuck what car you came in," Roy said.

I looked at Hawk. He shrugged.

"When's the last time you saw Mary Smith?" I said.

"Mary who?"

I sighed.

"Mary Toricelli," I said.

"Why?"

"Why not?" I said.

"I don't know when I seen her, all right?"

"Not all right," I said. "I've been told that you and she are still intimate."

"Huh?"

"He mean you and she still fucking," Hawk said gently. "He just talk kind of funny."

"Hey," Levesque said. "That's no way to talk about somebody."

"Just trying to find a language you're comfortable with," I said. "What about you and Mary?"

"Who told you that?"

"People who know," I said.

"So if they know so fucking much, how come you're asking me?"

"I like to confirm at the source."

"Huh?"

"He mean ask the one fucking her," Hawk said.

"Hey, pal, watch your freaking mouth," Levesque said.

Hawk looked at me. "Pal," he said.

I nodded. "Limited vocabulary," I said. "I'm sure he meant no harm."

"Hey, I'm trying to work here," Levesque said. "You guys are on private property."

"Oh my," Hawk said.

Levesque glanced at Hawk. Hawk made him uneasy.

"My boss sees me talking like this, I could get fired."

I looked around. We were near the corner of a big corrugated-metal lumber shed.

I said to Levesque, "Let's go around the corner then."

Hawk took hold of his left arm and I his right and we moved him pretty quickly around the corner so we were standing out of sight between the back of the warehouse and a hill full of weeds. We banged him hard against the back of the shed, and stepped back.

"What's going on with you and Mary," I said.

Levesque put his hand under his shirttail and came out with a gun. It was a squat black semiautomatic.

"You motherfuckers get away from me," he said.

Hawk smiled. "You not saying it right," he said. "Correct pronunciation be muthafuckas."

The gun wasn't cocked. On a semiautomatic you have to cock it for the first shot.

"Look at me," I said.

He looked and Hawk took the gun out of his hand. Hawk is very quick.

"Don't see so many of these," Hawk said. "Forty-caliber."

"Forty?"

"Yep."

"For crissake," I said.

I put my hand out. Hawk gave me the gun and as he did, Levesque turned and ran.

"You want him?" Hawk said.

I shook my head. I was looking at the gun.

"Nathan Smith was killed with a forty-caliber slug," I said.

"There's more than one forty-caliber around," Hawk said.

"I know," I said. "Still, most people don't own one. Most people buy thirty-eights or -nines."

"If he bought it," Hawk said.

"Still a large coincidence," I said. "Smith's killed by a sort of unusual gun and one of the principals turns up with a gun that's the same kind of sort of unusual."

"Gonna take it to Quirk," Hawk said.

"I am."

"Then we know," Hawk said.

CHAPTER FORTY-EIGHT

I had a picture of Marvin Conroy that Rita had gotten me from the Pequod Bank. Race Witherspoon and I took the picture down to Nellie's and showed it to the third-floor bartender, whose name was Rick. The place was nearly empty. Two or three guys sat around at separate tables, and a party of four were drinking tequila sunrises at a round table near the stairs.

Rick was a tall thin guy with his thinning hair cut very short. He wore round eyeglasses with gold frames. There was a blue-and-red sea serpent tattooed on his left forearm. He looked at the picture of Conroy for a while, then looked at Race.

"He's cool," Race said.

I smiled in a cool way. Rick studied me for a minute.

"Yeah, he was in here."

"You remember him?"

"Yeah, sure. He was a straight guy, and he was asking me about Nathan Smith. And he had attitude."

"How could you tell he was straight?" I said.

Rick looked at me and snorted.

"Oh," I said. "That's how. What did you tell him?"

"I told him I didn't know Nathan Smith."

"He press you?"

"Yes."

"He say what he wanted?"

"No. I thought he might be some detective Smith's wife hired."

"Why?"

"Some of the men who come in here, they're married and their wives are starting to wonder about them."

"He ask about Nathan's sex life?"

Rick shook his head. "Just wanted to know if he came in here often."

"If he came here often," Race said, "you wouldn't have to ask about his sex life. It's why people come here often."

"Looking for young men," I said.

"The younger the better."

"So if you knew Smith came here often, you'd surmise he was gay."

Rick looked at me. "And you'd probably know the Pope was Catholic," he said.

"He talk with anybody else?" I said.

"He tried."

"And?"

"Nobody here is going to talk with a guy like that."

"He hang around?" I said.

"Yeah. I got off work early one night," Rick said, "and I saw him outside."

"What was he doing?"

"Just sitting in his car outside the club. Another car went by in the other direction and the headlights shined on him."

"Was Nathan Smith here the night this guy was outside?" I said.

"I don't know . . . yes he was. Because I thought, 'I wonder if he's waiting for Nathan.' "

"Which he was," Race said.

I nodded. "And whom he probably saw," I said.

"So he knew he was queer," Race said.

"Conroy must have had some reason to think Smith was queer," I said. "Otherwise why would he come here?"

"And why here?" Race said. "Why not visit all the many gay places, the come-what-may places?"

"Maybe he did."

"We can ask," Race said.

"You know them all?"

"Known them all already," Race said, "known them all."

"Strayhorn," I said, "and Eliot in the same conversation."

"I'm not just another pretty face," Race said.

We spent the next eight hours moving from gay bar to gay bar. No one else had encountered Marvin Conroy that they could remember. Near midnight we sat at the bar of a place in the South End called Ramrod and drank beer.

"So Conroy had an idea what he'd find out before he went to Nellie's," I said.

"Apparently," Race said. "He doesn't seem to have gone anywhere else."

"Have we missed any?"

"None that a guy like Conroy would have known about," Race said.

"So who told him?" I said.

"Am I a detective," Race said.

"I'm beginning to wonder the same thing about me," I said.

CHAPTER

FORTY-NINE

Quirk called me in the morning, at home, while I was still lying in bed thinking about orange juice.

"The gun you gave me killed Nathan Smith," Quirk said.

"Better to be lucky than good," I said.

"Good to be both," Quirk said. "Franklin cops picked up Levesque last night. Belson and I are going out to talk with him. Want to ride along?"

"Yes."

"Be out front of your place in half an hour."

I had time for orange juice and a shower. As I went out my front door I was thinking of coffee. Belson was driving. Quirk sat up front beside him. I got in the back. Quirk handed me a cup of coffee over the seat back. Salvation.

"Where's Hawk?"

"I figured I'd be safe with you guys," I said.

"Serve and protect," Quirk said.

"You got anything on DeRosa yet?"

"Nope. Slugs came from two different guns. Nine-millimeter and forty-five. Both guns shot both people. Often."

"How many rounds?"

"Twenty-seven."

"Sure did want them dead," I said.

"Maybe they liked the work," Belson said.

"Maybe he had two guns," I said.

"Whichever," Belson said.

I drank my coffee.

We talked to Levesque in a cell at the Franklin Police Station. He didn't think he was tough anymore. He sat on the bunk in jeans and an undershirt, no belt and no shoelaces, hunched forward, his forearms resting limply against his thighs, his hands dangling. Quirk stood in front of him, hands in his pockets, all the time in the world. Belson leaned on one wall. I leaned on the other. A Franklin cop stood outside the cell, with a guy from the Norfolk County DA's office.

Quirk said, "You know who I am, Roy?"

He sounded friendly. Levesque nodded.

"You know why you're here?"

"Something about a gun," Levesque mumbled.

Quirk nodded at me.

"This good citizen took a gun away from you that was used to kill a man in Boston."

"I didn't kill no one."

"I believe you, Roy. And I know Sergeant Belson believes you, and I'm pretty sure Mr. Spenser believes you. But I'm not positive that the assistant DA believes you. And I'm not sure a judge and jury would believe you, and I'm not so sure but that you might go down for it."

"Honest to God, sir, I didn't kill nobody."

Quirk nodded thoughtfully and hit Levesque with his open hand hard, across the face. Quirk is a big man. Levesque rocked back and almost fell. He put both hands up on top of his head and tried to hide behind his forearms.

"Don't lie to me," Quirk said to Levesque without emotion.

Belson said, "Captain."

The assistant DA, whose name was Santoro, said, "Captain, Jesus Christ."

Quirk ignored them. He said, "Tell me about the gun, Roy."

Levesque kept his arms up, protecting his face.

"I don't know anything," he said.

Quirk smiled and leaned forward and slapped Levesque hard on the back of the head. Levesque moved his hands to try to protect himself and doubled up, his elbows touching his knees.

Santoro said, "Captain, we can't have that. I don't know what you do in Boston, but in Norfolk County, we can't have that."

Quirk paid no attention. He said, "Tell me about the gun, Roy."

The Franklin cop said, "I don't want to be a part of this."

"You're right," Santoro said. "I don't either."

They both turned and walked down the corridor.

"I'm sorry, Captain," Belson said. "No disrespect, but I can't watch this."

"Me either," I said.

Quirk said nothing. Levesque huddled on his bunk. Belson and I went out of the cell and closed the door. I saw Levesque hunch his shoulders up a little tighter. I followed Belson down the hallway.

"Coffee in the squad room," the Franklin cop said.

We went in. Santoro was there already, sitting at the end of a Formica table with a cup of coffee. Belson and I got some and sat at the table with him. He had gotten the last donut. The empty box sat evocatively on the table.

"I hear you know Rita Fiore," Santoro said.

"You work for the Norfolk DA when she was there?" I said.

Santoro looked reminiscent. "I did," he said.

"I'm working for her now," I said.

"Getting any fringe benefits?" Santoro said.

"Rita and I are friends," I said with dignity.

"And Rita's got no enemies," Santoro said.

"How long you think," the Franklin cop said.

Belson looked at his watch. "Usually goes quick."

"Seriously," Santoro said, "you ever give Rita a little bop?"

"In my case it would be a big bop," I said. "And it's not your business."

"Hey, just killing a little time."

"Kill it another way," I said.

Santoro shrugged. We drank our coffee.

After a while, Belson said, "I don't think it would be such a big bop."

"I don't wish to discuss it," I said.

"I'll check it with Susan," Belson said.

"She's promised not to tell," I said.

The door to the squad room opened and Quirk stuck his head in.

"Levesque wants to make a statement," Quirk said.

CHAPTER FIFTY

Levesque's statement was sort of complete, but the essence of it was that his old friend Mary Toricelli Smith had given him the gun to dispose of, and he had kept it instead.

"Said he'd never had a gun," Quirk told us on the ride back to Boston. "Said he held on to it because he'd always wanted one and maybe it would come in handy someday."

"It came in handy for someone," I said.

"Levesque says he was Mary Toricelli's boyfriend, before and after she married Smith. Says that Mr. and Mrs. Smith had an open marriage. Smith with boys, her with him, Levesque."

"We believe his story?"

"Sounded true to me," Quirk said.

"Too scared to lie?"

"Be my guess," Quirk said.

"They coulda been in it together," Belson said.

"Sure."

"She denies it, it'll be her word against his."

"Prints?" I said.

"His," Quirk said, and smiled. "Hawk's. Nothing else we can use. Gun's been handled a lot."

"Powder residue?"

"Too long ago," Quirk said.

"Smith had ten million dollars' life insurance."

"Coulda killed him for his money," Belson said. "And when everything died down, she moves the boyfriend in."

"You had Smith's money," Quirk said, "would you move Roy Levesque in?"

"He ain't my type," Belson said. "But it seems like he was hers."

"He say how Mary Toricelli met Nathan Smith?" I said.

"He didn't say."

"Might be good to know," I said.

"I'll get to it," Quirk said.

"So where does all the other stuff fit?" I said.

"Like?"

"Like Brinkman the broker, and Amy Peters, and Soldiers Field Development, and Marvin Conroy, and the kid I killed in Southie, and Jack DeRosa and his girlfriend, for instance," I said.

"You always been picky," Quirk said.

"You ask him any of that?"

"I'll get to it."

"We going to talk with her?" I said.

"We? All of a sudden it's we?"

"I want to make sure you don't start whacking her in the face," I said.

"I'm going to call her attorney," Quirk said. "Have her come in with Mrs. Smith for a dignified interview."

"Homicide commander doesn't usually get down to this level of nitty-gritty," I said. "Does he? Or she?"

"In this case, he," Quirk said. "Lotta people been killed. And the suspect is worth a large amount of money."

"So you're hearing about it."

"Mayor's up for reelection," Quirk said. "He's been bragging about the crime rate."

"So you're showing a laudable hands-on interest."

Quirk nodded. He might have almost smiled a little.

"And there are personnel issues," he said.

Belson kept his eyes on the road as he spoke over his right shoulder.

"I told Quirk I'd take early retirement," he said, "before I'd go one-on-one with Mary Smith again."

"The power of dumb," I said.

CHAPTER FIFTY-ONE

When I got back to my office there were two calls on my answering machine. One was from Hawk asking if I still needed backup. The other was from a secretary at Kiley and Harbaugh. Mr. Kiley would like to have breakfast with me in the coffee shop of his building the next morning and could I call to confirm. I called Hawk at the Harbor Health Club and left a message with Henry that since everybody seemed to have skedaddled, and whatever was going on had stopped, I figured there was no further need to kill me and Hawk could therefore go back to his career of crime. Then I called the secretary at Kiley and Harbaugh and confirmed, and, at 7:30 the next morning, I met him there. He was already seated when I came in.

"Don't have the bagels," Kiley said. "Cranberry muffins."

I went to the counter and got orange juice, coffee, and a cranberry muffin and brought it to Kiley's table, and sat. Kiley didn't say anything. I drank some juice. Kiley had a muffin, too, and some juice. Same breakfast I was having, except I was eating mine.

"I been practicing criminal law around here for most of my adult life," Kiley said.

I drank some orange juice

"I known you sort of here and there and roundabout for a long time," Kiley said.

I nodded and drank the rest of my orange juice.

"Everything I know about you says your word is good."

"For something," I said.

"I checked on you, cops, DA, lotta people." Kiley smiled. "Some of them clients. The consensus is that you're a hard-on, but I can trust you."

I had mixed feelings about the consensus, but I had nothing to add.

"Before we talk," Kiley said, "I need your word that it goes no further."

"I can't promise, Bobby, until I know what I'm promising."

Kiley looked at my face for a moment and pursed his lips. His cranberry muffin lay on his plate unmolested.

"It's about my daughter," he said.

I put a little milk in my coffee and stirred it. "I'll protect your daughter," I said carefully, "if I can."

"What makes you think she needs protection?" Kiley said.

"Come on, Bobby."

He nodded. "Yeah. That was dumb. Okay. You gimme your word?"

"I'll do the best I can," I said.

"Your word?"

"Yes."

"The kid you killed," Kiley said.

"Kevin McGonigle."

"Yeah. We represented him once."

I raised my eyebrows. I could raise one at a time, but I saved that for women.

"Him and another guy, guy named Scanlan, got arrested on assault charges. They beat up a real estate appraiser. Cops caught them in progress, down back of South Station."

"Why?"

"Appraiser claims he didn't know them, had no idea why they assaulted him. Refused to press charges."

Kiley was right about the cranberry muffins.

"So how'd you get involved?" I said.

"Guy called here, asked us to go down and see about them. We represented them maybe two hours."

"They call you?"

"No. Ann took it."

"She go down?"

"Yes."

"What was the appraiser's name?" I said.

Kiley took a piece of folded notepaper from his shirt pocket and read it.

"Bisbee," he said. "Thomas Bisbee."

He handed me the paper.

"Who paid you?"

"That's bothersome," Kiley said. "We got no record of anybody paying us."

"Any record of anybody being billed?"

"No."

"That is bothersome," I said. "McGonigle didn't look like your kind of client any more than DeRosa did."

"We're criminal lawyers," Kiley said. "Some of our clients are criminals."

"Usually criminals who can pay."

"True."

"Was McGonigle someone who could pay?"

"He wasn't. He was muscle. Just like Scanlan."

"Who were they working for?" I said.

"I don't know."

I got up and went to the serving counter and got more coffee for myself and a fresh cup for Kiley.

"So," I said when I came back, "what do you want from me?"

"I want to know how deep in she is," Kiley said.

"You asked her?"

"She won't talk to me about it. She says it's a question of profes-sional respect, that she won't allow me to treat her like a child."

"And you want me to find out what happened," I said.

"Goddamn it, she's *my* child."

I nodded. "I have a client," I said.

"I'm not asking you anything that would interfere with that. I'm asking you while you're serving your client to keep an eye out. And let me know."

"Give me the name of the other guy she defended."

"Chuckie Scanlan."

"Chuck," I said.

"You know him?"

"No. Guy named Jack DeRosa claimed a guy named Chuck put him in touch with Mary Smith."

"Common name," Kiley said.

I nodded. "Where do I find him?"

"Works in a liquor store on Broadway. Donovan's."

"Ann knows this guy, she knew DeRosa, and she is, or was, Marvin Conroy's girlfriend."

"Yeah. I noticed that, too," Kiley said.

"Ann know where Conroy is?" I said.

"She says she doesn't."

"We may be going in the same direction," I said. "I'll do what I can."

"And report to me."

"Anything I find out about Ann, I'll report to you first."

"Only," Kiley said.

"Bobby, what if she's in too far?"

"She's my only child, Spenser. Her mother's dead."

"I can't promise, Bobby. I can walk away from this conversation and say nothing to anybody. But I can't promise you more than I can promise you."

"You going to talk with Chuckie Scanlan?"

"Yes."

"And if that leads you someplace and Ann's in it really deep?"

"Then I'll talk to you," I said.

"Before you talk to anyone else?"

"Yes."

"And what?" Kiley said.

"And we'll decide," I said.

FIFTY-TWO

It was a hot day and there was no air moving. Donovan's Liquors was a big store with a big sign in the window that advertised the coldest beer in Boston. There was a burly woman with big brass-colored hair at the cash register when I went in.

"Chuckie Scanlan?" I said to her.

"He's out back."

"Mind if I go back and see him?" I said.

"Who are you?"

"New caseworker," I said. "Wanted to say hello."

It was a vague enough term to cover several jobs and I figured Chuckie would be covered by one of them. The big woman made an ushering sweep with her right hand and pointed me toward the back room. Chuckie was stacking cases of Budweiser. He was a short wide guy with very little hair.

"Chuckie Scanlan?"

"Yeah?"

"My name's Spenser. We need to talk."

Scanlan's eyes showed a moment of something and then went dead again.

"About what?"

"You, Kevin McGonigle."

"Kevin's dead," Scanlan said.

"And you're not," I said, "yet."

"Whaddya mean?"

"We need to talk," I said.

Scanlan jerked his head and we went out the back door into the heavy air and sat on a pile of wooden skids in the near corner of the narrow parking lot behind the store. Scanlan lit a cigarette.

"You a cop?" he said.

"Private," I said. "I came from Bobby Kiley's office."

"Kiley?"

"Kiley and Harbaugh. They represented you a couple years ago."

"Oh, yeah. The broad came down, got us sprung. Cops had nothing."

"Broad's name was probably Ann," I said.

"Yeah, Ms. Kiley. Good-looking. Smart as hell," Scanlan said. "How come you're talking about me not being dead, yet?"

"You know Marvin Conroy?"

Scanlan took in some smoke and let it out slowly, squinting through it at me. "Conroy?"

"Un-huh."

"I never met him. I think he was a friend of Jack's."

"Jack?" I said.

"DeRosa," Scanlan said.

Bingo!

"How'd you know DeRosa?" I said.

"He hired me and Kevin to do some stuff."

"For Conroy?"

"I guess."

"You know what happened to McGonigle?" I said.

"I heard Kevin got it in a shootout over on A Street."

"From me," I said.

"Huh?"

"He got it from me. I shot him."

Scanlan took in some more smoke. I knew so few people who smoked anymore that it was kind of fascinating to watch him.

"How come you shot him?"

"He was trying to shoot me," I said.

Scanlan shrugged. "Shit happens," he said.

"Tell me about Marvin Conroy."

"Nothing to tell," Scanlan said. "When the cops tried to hang me with that bum rap he helped me out with the lawyer."

"Why?" I said.

"I guess he was the one got Jack to hire us."

"To do what?"

Scanlan said, "A little of this, a little of that."

"You're a thug," I said. "You were doing strong-arm work."

"Cops couldn't hold us."

"Somebody shot Jack DeRosa to pieces," I said.

"Jack?"

"Jack and his girlfriend," I said. "Fifty rounds."

"Margy?"

"Yep."

"Why her?"

"Probably for being there."

"Who done it?"

"What would be your guess?" I said.

"How the fuck would I know?"

"I figure Jack got it because he knew something and somebody wanted to make sure he didn't tell it to me."

"You?"

"Yeah," I said. "I figure you know it, too."

"They killed him so he wouldn't talk with you?"

"Seems like."

"So?"

"Now I'm talking to you," I said.

Scanlan looked around the parking area.

"You son of a bitch," he said.

I smiled at him.

"You're setting me up."

"No," I said. "I'm asking you about Marvin Conroy."

"Why him?"

"Detective's intuition," I said.

"And if I don't know nothing about him?"

"I keep hanging around and asking about him and talking to you and talking to other people about talking to you."

"You bastard, you're going to get me killed."

"Not if you tell me what you know."

Scanlan glanced around the lot again. There were only two cars parked there.

"You got a gun," Scanlan said.

"I do."

"What happens if I remembered some stuff?" Scanlan said.

"I go away and never mention your name again," I said.

Scanlan dropped his cigarette and stepped on it and got out a package of Marlboros and lit a new one.

"I don't know much," he said.

I waited.

"Jack DeRosa come to me and Kevin one day, says he's got a easy couple a hundred for us. Tells me all we got to do is rough up some fucking suit. So we say why not, and he says the guy comes down Summer Street every night, same time, got a condo over by the milk bottle thing, you know? And we say fine, we'll pull him over behind the Postal Annex and have our talk."

Scanlan dragged in some smoke.

"So the next night, Jack drives us over there and points out the guy. He waits in the car, and we go over and do it. But while we're doing it some fucking postal cop comes by and pulls his gun. Once in a lifetime, you know, I mean, how many postal cops you ever seen, for crissake. Jack takes off, and we're busted. EMTs show up and patch our guy up and we all go over to the station and me and Kevin are shutting up because, what the fuck, we don't even know why we're smacking the guy around."

"DeRosa tell you to say anything to him?"

"Jack says just tell him it's a message from his bank."

"He seem to understand that?"

"Who knows. He's so fucking scared it's hard to say what he understood. So we're in the station and the cops are yelling at us and we're saying jack shit, and this lady lawyer comes in. Man, I'd fuck her in a heartbeat."

"She'll be pleased to know that," I said.

"She tells us her name and says she's from Kiley and Harbaugh. She says that the suit won't bring charges, and that she's getting us released."

He stopped his eyes moving back and forth across the parking lot.

"That's it?" I said.

"Yeah."

"You never saw her again?"

"No."

"Where's Marvin Conroy come in?" I said.

"Oh, him," Scanlan said. "Jack picks us up after we're out, and I say to Jack, 'Thanks for sending us a lawyer,' and he says, 'No problem,' and I say, 'We owe anybody any money?' and he says, 'Nope, it's on Marvin Conroy,' and I say, 'Who's Marvin Conroy?' And Jack kind of smiles and says, 'The guy from the bank.' "

"You know who sent McGonigle to kill me?"

"No idea."

"You driving the car?"

"No way."

"Jack DeRosa send you?"

"I wasn't there, man. DeRosa was in jail then."

"How do you know when it happened?"

"Kevin was a friend of mine," Scanlan said. "I remember when he got killed."

"DeRosa send McGonigle?"

"Could be," Scanlan said.

I nodded. I didn't believe he wasn't driving, but I didn't think he knew much more than he'd told me. He was too far down the food chain. And I was pretty sure he wouldn't admit to being an accomplice to attempted murder. So I let it go.

"Okay," I said. "We're done."

"What'd you tell Barb?"

"At the checkout counter? I said I was your new caseworker."

Scanlan nodded. "She knows I done time," he said. "You gonna keep your mouth shut about this like you said?"

"Like a stone," I said.

CHAPTER

FIFTY-THREE

Susan's eyes were big and dark and brilliant with interest. "You think Ann Kiley recruited this DeRosa man?"

"Yes."

"If Marvin Conroy and Ann Kiley are so deeply in love that she'll supply thugs, and bail them out afterwards," Susan said, "would he leave without a word and she not know where he was?"

"Maybe she was the only one deeply in love," I said.

"Maybe," Susan said. "But it might be worth keeping an eye on her."

I smiled, and said, "Great idea."

Susan studied my face for a moment. "You're already doing that, aren't you?"

I shrugged.

"Not Hawk," Susan said. "He's watching you."

I shrugged again.

"Vinnie?"

"Yeah."

"Vinnie is watching Ann Kiley."

"I thought it would be good if we knew where she went and who she talked to, and maybe offer a little protection."

"I thought her father was arranging protection."

"He was, but, you know, Vinnie is pretty good."

"Depends how you define good," Susan said.

"He's the best shooter I ever saw," I said.

"That's how I thought you'd define it," Susan said.

I was on a stool in Susan's kitchen, supervising as she made egg salad for sandwiches. She was spooning Miracle Whip into a bowl with the hard-boiled eggs. Pearl was lying on her couch across the room, aging, but still alert to the possibility of a spoon to lick.

"I didn't know they made Miracle Whip anymore," I said.

"They do."

"Many people use mayo," I said.

"Miracle Whip makes a much better egg salad," she said.

I nodded.

"You ever think of mixing in some chopped green peppers?" I said.

"No," she said.

"I like a person clear on their preferences," I said.

"Me too. Have you found any intersection between Mary Smith and the Levesque person on one hand, and Conroy and Ann Kiley and that group on the other?"

"Nathan Smith," I said.

"Besides that," Susan said.

"No."

"Maybe there isn't one," she said.

"Sometimes I snip a few chives into the egg salad," I said.

"I don't," she said. She stirred some chopped celery into the egg and Miracle Whip mixture.

"You think she killed her husband?"

"Looks like it," I said. "The gun she gave Levesque to get rid of is the one that killed him."

"Do you think Marvin Conroy is the one who killed all these other people?"

"He's involved," I said. "Soldiers Field Development might have something to do with it, too."

"To do with what?" Susan said.

She spread out five slices of white bread and began to spread each with her egg-salad mixture.

"White bread?" I said.

"You eat egg salad on white bread," Susan said. "What is it that Conroy and Soldiers Field had something to do with?"

"I don't know. Something, I would guess, to do with real estate and mortgage money fraud."

"Because it's a bank and a development company."

"Because of that," I said. "I still need to talk with the guy that got beat up, Bisbee."

"He was a real estate person," Susan said.

She put a leaf of Bibb lettuce on each of the five egg-covered bread slices.

"Yeah. And Amy Peters was in banking, and Brink Tyler was a financial advisor, and Nathan Smith was a banker. And he was on the board of Soldiers Field Development, and they've disappeared, and he brought Marvin Conroy into the bank, and Marvin Conroy was Ann Kiley's boyfriend, and he's disappeared, and Ann Kiley represented Jack DeRosa, who lied that Mary Smith hired him to kill her husband, and who hired Chuckie Scanlan to beat up Thomas Bisbee and probably to kill me, and Ann represented him, too, and Conroy was investigating Nathan Smith's sexuality, and Larson Graff was a friend of Nathan's, and a boyhood friend of Mary's and Roy Levesque, and Mary says she met Nathan through Graff, and Graff says he met Nathan because of Mary, and . . ."

"Jesus Christ," Susan said. "You're giving me a headache."

"Lot of that going around," I said.

Susan completed her five sandwiches with five more slices of white bread, then she cut them into cute quarters and put them on a small platter. Beside the sandwiches, artfully, she put a few cherry tomatoes and some cornichons.

"There's a bottle of Riesling in the refrigerator," Susan said. "If you'll bring it out onto the back porch we'll have lunch."

I put the wine in an ice bucket, got two glasses and a corkscrew, and followed Susan. Pearl dragged off the couch and limped after us to the porch. It was a lovely August day. We sat at Susan's little filigreed glass-topped table. Pearl sat beside Susan. Susan gave her a quarter of a sandwich.

"How," Susan said, "on earth are you going to unravel all of that?"

I uncorked the bottle.

"Same way you do therapy," I said.

"Which is?"

"Find a thread, follow it where it leads, and keep on doing it."

"Sometimes it leads to another thread."

"Often," I said.

"And then you follow that thread."

"Yep."

I ate a bite of my sandwich. Miracle Whip maybe was good in an egg salad sandwich. Susan nibbled on a cornichon. I sipped some Riesling. I liked Riesling.

"Like a game," Susan said.

"For both of us," I said.

Susan nodded. "Yes," she said, "the tracking down of a person or an idea or an evasion."

"Or fixing something that's broken," I said. "Like home repair."

"Or both," Susan said. "Except sometimes it's awfully hard."

"Part of its charm," I said.

"I know. I know. Can't win if there's no chance of losing. It's true," Susan said. "But not consoling in the moment."

"No," I said. "Not in the moment."

Susan gave Pearl another quarter of the extra sandwich she'd made. Pearl chomped it briskly and wagged her tail.

"Speaking of consolation in the moment," I said

"She's easily consoled," Susan said.

CHAPTER FIFTY-FOUR

The seven of us met in a conference room down the hall from Quirk's office. Rita was there, and me, Belson and Quirk, a guy named Russo from Owen Brooks's office, and Mary Smith and Larson Graff. We were seated in gray metal chairs around a gray metal table. Larson sat on one side of Mary, and Rita was on the other. Rita had a yellow notepad in front of her. Russo had one in front of him. It was how they knew they were lawyers. There was a tape recorder on the table. Quirk turned it on and explained the date and the people in attendance.

"Spenser is here as Ms. Fiore's investigator," Quirk said to Mary Smith. "He has no police status."

"I think he used to be a policeman," Mary said.

Quirk ignored her. "Mr. Graff here also has no status in this proceeding."

"I don't see why . . ." Mary Smith began.

Rita put a hand on her arm and shook her head. Mary stopped talking.

"We have the weapon that killed your husband," Quirk said. "A forty-caliber Smith and Wesson semiautomatic pistol."

Mary smiled at him.

"Ohmigod," she said. "I don't know anything about guns."

"It was taken by our friend Spenser here, from a man named Roy Levesque."

"Roy had it?"

"You know Roy Levesque," Quirk said.

"Sure, I mean of course, we went to high school together."

"When did you last see him?" Quirk said.

"Oh, I really, really . . . I see so many people. All the time. I'm really a people person, I guess."

"Levesque says you gave him the gun."

"Roy said that?"

"Yes."

"Why did he say that?" Mary said.

"Did you give him the gun?"

"Not to keep," Mary said.

Mary was confused. She turned and gazed at Larson Graff, as if maybe Larson knew and would help her out with the hard questions. Larson didn't look at her.

"Did you give him the gun? And tell him to get rid of it?" Quirk said again. There was no threat or anger in his voice. He seemed perfectly patient about it.

"I think maybe my client and I need to talk a little," Rita said.

Quirk nodded toward the door, and Rita took Mary outside and closed the door and stayed in the hall with her for maybe ten minutes. While we waited Quirk turned to Graff.

"So, Larson," Quirk said. "You think Levesque is telling the truth?"

"I really have no idea, Captain."

"So what was it you were doing here?"

"I came at Mrs. Smith's request."

"She take you everywhere?" Quirk said.

"There's no need for attitude, Captain. Mary is much more at ease in any situation if I'm with her."

"You think she might have killed her husband?" Quirk said.

"My God, Captain. I don't know anything about that."

"Lucky she brought you," Quirk said.

No one spoke. Russo doodled on his yellow pad. Graff fidgeted, looking hopefully at the doorway through which Mary had disappeared. Quirk sat quietly looking at nothing. Belson watched Graff watch the door. The door opened after a while and Rita brought Mary back in. They sat. Quirk waited quietly.

"Are you planning to arrest my client?" Rita said.

"We might," Quirk said.

"We might be prepared to make a statement if there was something in it for us."

Quirk looked at Russo.

"What are you looking for?" Russo said.

"If, and this is hypothetical, in her statement Mrs. Smith admitted to a minor crime, she would not be prosecuted for it."

"How about the murder of her husband," Quirk said.

"If she made a statement, it would clarify that issue, and make it moot."

"The deal would depend on what she had to tell us," Russo said.

"If it is useful information, do we have a deal?"

"The deal being?" Russo said.

"No prosecution for any crime she might admit in her statement."

They then spent five minutes talking incomprehensibly about misdemeanors and C felonies and gobbledygook, while I looked at various parts of the room and found all of them equally uninteresting.

Finally Russo said, "Deal."

Rita nodded at Mary Smith. "Go ahead, Mary. Tell them."

"What should I tell them?" Mary said.

"What you told me in the hall."

"Can't you tell them for me?"

"I think they'd rather hear it from you."

Mary sat frowning. She looked at Graff again. He didn't look back.

"Well . . . please don't all of you look at me. I get really, really, really nervous if everybody looks at me."

Nobody said anything. No one looked away. Mary licked her lips and looked at Larson again and then at Rita. Rita nodded encouragingly. I had known Rita a long time. I knew she wanted to jump up, take Mary by the neck, and shake her like a dust mop, but to the unpracticed eye Rita's nod looked supportive and kind.

"Well, I really . . . Nathan wasn't as rich as everybody thinks he was," Mary said.

She looked around at us. None of us spoke.

"Some kind of trouble at the bank, I think," Mary said. "And he would always tell me even if things got bad, I'd be all right because he had so much life insurance."

"How much?" Russo said.

"Ten million dollars."

"A lot," Russo said.

"And when I came in and found him."

"Found him?"

"Dead. Really, all I could think about was that insurance companies won't pay off on suicide."

"Suicide?" Quirk said.

"Yes. I thought, my God, I won't get a dime."

"Why did you think it was suicide," Quirk said.

"Well, I mean, really, there he was, the gun was right beside his hand."

"Gun?"

"Yes. That gun you were talking about, the forty-something or other. The one I gave to Roy."

"You found your husband dead?" Russo said. "With a gun by his side and you took the gun and gave it to Roy Levesque?"

"Yes."

"And you wanted him to get rid of it?" Quirk said.

"Yes. I didn't want the insurance company to know. I needed the money."

Everyone in the room was quiet.

"How long had he held the policy?" Russo said.

"He said he had it since he was a small boy."

"You check the policy?" Russo said.

"Oh, no. I really, really don't read things like that. They're really . . ."

Russo nodded and looked at Rita as he spoke to Mary.

"Most policies have an exclusion period, generally two years," Russo said. "After that they pay off on suicide like any other death."

Mary stared at him as if he were speaking in tongues. "I needed the money," she said.

I saw Rita sneak a long breath of air. "Okay?" she said to Quirk.

Quirk looked at me. "You got anything to offer?" he said.

"What kind of trouble was going on at the bank?" I said.

"Oh, I really don't know anything about that kind of thing," Mary said. "He brought Mr. Conroy in to help fix it."

I nodded. "You don't know where Conroy is now, do you?"

"At the bank, I guess."

"Just while we're all here," I said, "could I clean up one other little confusion? How'd you meet your husband, Mrs. Smith?"

She smiled at Larson Graff.

"Larson introduced us," she said.

"So he knew your husband prior to your marriage?"

"Excuse me?"

"Graff and your husband knew each other before you married your husband," I said.

"Oh, yes, of course."

I looked at Graff and waited. He was looking alertly at the table-top. Nobody else spoke.

"That so?" I said to Larson.

"I don't, I guess . . ." He frowned at the table. "I don't really re-call."

"You told me that you met him because he called you on behalf of his wife," I said.

"I didn't . . . I . . ."

Graff looked at Quirk. "I just don't think this is about me," Graff said.

Quirk nodded.

"Do I have to answer his questions?" Graff said.

"Nope."

"Well then, I won't."

"So," Quirk said. "Did you know Smith before he was married or not?"

"I don't remember."

"Mrs. Smith?" Quirk said.

"What?"

"Did Mr. Graff introduce you to your husband?"

"Yes. I told you that."

"He says he didn't."

"Larson, you did, too," Mary said. "You called me up and told me you had a rich friend that wanted to be married, and it was Nathan."

Graff didn't say anything.

"Larson," Mary said. "You did."

"Do I have to stay here?" Graff said.

Nobody responded. Graff looked around the table for a moment. Then he stood and left the room.

"Well, my God," Mary said. "What's wrong with him?"

"Maybe a lot," I said.

CHAPTER FIFTY-FIVE

Thomas Bisbee, wearing a yellow hard hat, was standing in the middle of a big building lot where three foundations were being poured. Since I hadn't seen anything that could fall on my head when I had parked on the street and started in, I risked the area without a hard hat. Bisbee had a clipboard, too, and work boots, and a tape measure on his belt—everything necessary to look exactly like a general contractor. In fact, of course, he was simply an appraiser and could have worn an Armani suit for all the heavy lifting he was going to perform. But apparently he liked the look.

"My name is Spenser," I said. "I'm a detective working on a murder."

"So how can I help you?" Bisbee said.

"We need to talk," I said.

"About what?"

"Felton Shawcross," I said, "Soldiers Field Development, Nathan Smith, Marvin Conroy, Brinkman Tyler, Ann Kiley, Jack DeRosa."

If you don't know which bait to use you throw it all out and let the fish tell you. Bisbee stood stock-still.

After a pause he said, "Who?"

I repeated the names. He listened, his face grimly blank. When I finished, he said, "We can sit on that wall," and walked over and sat on a stone wall that had probably belonged to the old farmhouse that was being replaced. I sat beside him.

"What's this about Marvin Conroy?" he said.

"You tell me," I said.

"What makes you think I have something to tell?"

"Because Marvin had two guys beat you up a while ago, and you wouldn't press charges."

"I . . . They didn't really hurt me," he said.

"Because a postal cop came along and stopped them before they did," I said. "Why didn't you press charges?"

"I . . . What's this about a murder?"

"Four or five murders," I said.

"My God."

"Why didn't you press charges?" I said.

Across the open field a big cement truck had backed in against the foundation forms and begun to sluice a gray slurry of concrete into the first foundation. There were some dandelions in the field, and a few buttercups. The breeze riffled the surface of the uncut grass.

"I don't want to discuss it," Bisbee said.

He was a thin-faced man with a gray-streaked black mustache and goatee. I waited.

I said, "We're way past that, Mr. Bisbee. You're a material witness to a case of multiple homicide. You could be arrested."

I was careful not to say that I would arrest him, as I had been careful not to say I was a police detective. But misunderstanding was possible.

"God, Jesus!" he said.

"So why didn't you press charges?"

"If I tell you, would I still be arrested?"

"No," I said.

I wasn't exactly lying. His arrest was not contingent on him telling me anything.

"It was the woman lawyer," he said.

"Ann Kiley?"

"Yes. She said she represented the two men who attacked me, and that she also represented Marvin."

"Marvin Conroy?"

"Yes. And Marvin wanted me to drop the charges."

"And why did you care what Marvin wanted?"

He looked at me as if I had blasphemed. "He . . . Marvin is very dangerous."

"What was your relationship?" I said.

"With Marvin?"

"Yes."

Across the way three laborers were moving the cement chute. Two more guys watching. Good ratio, I thought.

"I appraised some property for him."

"And?"

"He didn't like the appraisal."

"Why not?"

"He wanted me to inflate the appraisal."

"So he could get a bigger loan?"

"Something like that."

"So why'd you get beat up, to make you change your appraisal?"

"No. To keep me from telling anybody. Marvin was up to something. Probably flipping real estate, maybe covering some real shaky loans. I don't know. But I told him that I was suspicious and the next day he sent me a message."

"The message being?"

"To keep my mouth shut."

Bisbee had thin hands. He was holding onto the clipboard with both of them so tightly that the knuckles were white.

"Which you did?"

"Yes . . . There was another name you mentioned. Soldiers Field Development."

"Yeah?"

"That was the company that was developing the property."

"That Conroy wanted you to appraise?"

"Yes."

"You know anything about Nathan Smith?"

"No."

"Any other names mean anything to you?"

"No."

Bisbee's shoulders were hunched and he was sitting stiffly on the stone wall as if it were cold. Which it wasn't. He hung on to his clipboard.

I took a card out of my wallet and tucked it into the breast pocket of his plaid shirt.

"Anyone threatens you," I said, "call me. I'll take care of it."

Bisbee nodded without looking at the card, or at me. Across the field the driver of the cement truck was hosing down the cement chute. Five men were watching. Bad ratio.

"Thanks for your help," I said.

Bisbee nodded again. I left.

CHAPTER FIFTY-SIX

I sat with Vinnie Morris in my car parked on the second level of a parking garage beside a hotel in downtown Worcester, near the Centrum. Almost everything in downtown Worcester was near the Centrum.

"She drove out here this morning with an overnight case," Vinnie said. "Checked in a little after one."

"Alone?"

"Alone."

"You see any sign of Conroy?"

"Nope."

I looked at the dashboard clock. It was 2:47. I didn't like digital clocks. Nice phrases like *quarter to three* were becoming obsolete.

"You'd recognize him?"

"Yep."

"He ever make you when you tailed him before?"

"Nope."

"Okay," I said. "I'll hang here. They'd both know me. You go to the lobby and sit around and try to look like a hotel guest."

"I'll read a newspaper," Vinnie said.

"Master of disguise," I said. "If she goes out, follow her. If Conroy comes in, follow him. Find out what room he goes to. You got a cell phone?"

"Yep."

I took out a business card and wrote my car-phone number on it and gave it to Vinnie.

"If they get together, stay with them and call me."

"Okay."

Vinnie got out and walked toward the stairwell. He moved very precisely. As if he'd been expertly crafted. He was medium-sized and liked Ivy League clothes. Except for the way he moved, he didn't look anywhere near as dangerous as he was. I let the motor idle so the car phone would work, and punched in a number. My status was rising. I got right through to Bobby Kiley.

"Your daughter has checked into a hotel in Worcester with an overnight bag," I said. "I'm waiting for Marvin Conroy to show."

"Which hotel," Kiley said.

I told him.

"I'll be there in an hour," he said.

"I don't want Conroy spooked," I said. "There's a hydrant across the street from the main lobby entrance. Park there and wait for me to find you. What are you driving?"

"Black Lexus sedan," Kiley said. "Vanity plates—L-A-W-M-A-N."

"It'll be me, or a guy named Vinnie Morris, who's almost as good as me."

"I'll be there," Kiley said. "Thanks."

We hung up. I couldn't find anything on the radio that was recognizably musical. I did not want to listen to the opinions expressed on the talk shows. I didn't want to tie up my car phone, so I couldn't call Susan up. When all else fails, think about the case.

I still didn't know exactly what was happening. The business about taking the gun so it would look like murder was just the kind of smart move a couple of morons like Mary Smith and Roy Levesque would choose. The fact that the finger of suspicion would then point at Mary, his heir, would never have occurred to them. Or it could be a double fake to cover up the fact that they really had killed him and Roy was too dumb to get rid of the gun.

But I did know that the only connection between what seemed like two separate cases, but probably wasn't, was Marvin Conroy. He was connected through the bank to the Smiths and Soldiers Field Development and that side. He was connected through Ann Kiley to Jack DeRosa and Chuckie Scanlan and that whole side, where people were getting killed. If I believed Bisbee, and there was no reason not to, Conroy and Soldiers Field and Pequod Bank were involved in some kind of swindle. The need for an inflated appraisal made me wonder if it was a land flip. But in wondering that, I exhausted my expertise. Rita would know. Or she would have somebody in the firm who would know.

At 4:53 my car phone rang.

"I'm on the seventh floor," Vinnie said. "She's in room 7112. He's in there with her."

"Here I come," I said.

As I headed for the stairs to the lobby I looked down and saw Bobby Kiley's Lexus. When I got to the seventh floor, Vinnie was standing outside the elevator, looking like a man waiting to go down.

"Turn right," Vinnie said. "Halfway down the corridor."

"He wonder about you when you rode up with him?"

"Maybe. But what's he going to do?"

I nodded.

"How you going to get in?" Vinnie said.

"Maybe I'll knock on the door, like in the movies, tell him there's a message?"

Vinnie grinned. "And he says slip it under the door."

"And I say he's got to sign for it."

"And the dope jumps up and opens the door."

"Or he tells me to blow," I said. "Especially if nobody knows he's here and how could they send him a message."

"Always works in the movies," Vinnie said.

"I can take it from here," I said to Vinnie.

"You don't want me to shoot nobody?"

"Thank you for asking," I said. "Another time."

"Sure."

"Guy named Bobby Kiley is parked across the street from the lobby entrance in a black Lexus sedan, vanity plates say 'Lawman.' Send him up and tell him I'll be outside the room or in it."

"Kiley," Vinnie said.

"Girl's father," I said.

Vinnie nodded. He pushed the button for the elevator. The door slid open. The same car I'd come up in was still there. Vinnie got in, pushed the button for the lobby, and the door slid shut. I walked down the hall to room 7112 and stood opposite the door and leaned on the wall and waited. I was still there when Bobby Kiley came down the corridor.

"Is he in there?" Kiley said.

"Yes."

"Have you knocked?"

"I was waiting for you."

Bobby Kiley took a deep breath and let it out slowly through his nose.

"I'll knock," he said.

FIFTY-SEVEN

It was probably two full minutes, and Kiley had knocked three times when Ann opened the door with the chain on.

"Daddy?"

"Open up, Ann," Kiley said. "We need to talk."

"Daddy, not now."

"Now, honey."

Through the narrow space produced by the barely opened door I could see Ann Kiley's eyes shift briefly to me, and back to her father.

"Daddy, I'm busy."

"I know," Kiley said. "And I know who you're busy with. Open the door, Annie."

"Daddy," she said, emphasizing the two syllables, stretching out the second one.

"Annie, you're a full-grown woman. Who you sleep with, and how often, is your business and not mine. But we're dealing with four or five murders here . . . and you're involved, and I am going to get you uninvolved. If we have to kick this thing in, we will."

I think he meant that I would. But it was not a time for quibbling over pronouns.

"I have to close it to take the chain off," Ann said.

Kiley nodded. The door closed. The chain bolt slid. The door opened and we went in. Ann was wearing a hotel-issue white terrycloth bathrobe. Her hair was mussed. Her clothes were haphazardly draped on the hard chair in front of the desk by the window. On the desk was a bottle of champagne and two glasses. The king-sized bed was still made, but it was badly rumpled and the pillows had been pulled out from under the spread. There was no one else in the room. But a man's clothes were carelessly folded on the armchair to the right of the door. I walked to the bathroom and opened the door. Marvin Conroy was standing behind the pebbled glass door in the shower stall with only his pants on, the belt still unbuckled.

"Who would think to look here," I said and held the shower door.

It is hard to look dignified when you're caught hiding in the shower with your pants unbuckled. Conroy did his best as he came out of the bathroom, but it didn't seem to me that he succeeded. He buckled his pants as inconspicuously as he could, and stepped into the brown loafers with the black highlights, which he had left neatly at the foot of the bed. Shirtless, he looked kind of soft, not fat exactly, but like a guy who makes his living shuffling money. I could tell he was holding his stomach in. He saw his shirt hanging on one arm of the soft chair and retrieved it and put it on, though he didn't tuck it in. As he dressed, he rejuvenated. By the time his shirt was buttoned he was nearly back to bank CEO. Ann sat on the side of the bed without a word. Her head was down, and she looked at nothing.

"Bobby," Conroy said. "What the hell are you doing?"

Kiley didn't say anything. He went to the bed and sat beside his daughter. Conroy fumbled with his cuff links. He turned his gaze from Kiley and focused it on me.

"And what the hell are you doing here?" he said.

He was getting tougher by the minute. By the time his cuff links were in he'd be threatening me. I leaned against the door.

"Here's what I've got," I said. "I know you were looking into Nathan Smith's sexual preferences."

"What the fuck are you talking about?" Conroy said.

"And I know you had Jack DeRosa hire a couple of mulligans to beat up a real estate appraiser named Bisbee to make sure he didn't tell anybody that you were asking him to inflate appraisals. And I know you got Jack DeRosa from Ann Kiley, and I know you got Ann to go down and straighten things out when the mulligans got arrested. And I know that you were in business with Soldiers Field Development, and I'm pretty sure I can prove that you were involved in some sort of land flip with them. You worked with Amy Peters. She's dead. You worked with Jack DeRosa. He's dead. You were snooping on Nathan Smith. He's dead. Sooner or later I'll tie you to Brinkman Tyler."

I stopped. Conroy was silent. I didn't blame him. There was a lot coming down. He didn't say, "Who's Brinkman Tyler," and he probably should have. After a moment, he stood.

"I'm leaving," he said firmly.

I shook my head. "No," I said. "You're not."

"Are you saying you'll prevent me?"

"Yes."

He stared at me, trying for outrage. He fell a little short. He was thinking about whether he could force me to let him go, and deciding that he couldn't. He was correct.

"You can't—"

"Sure I can," I said. "What we're trying to decide here is how much we can keep her out of it."

For the first time since he'd come out of the bathroom, Conroy looked at Ann.

"There's no *it* to keep anybody out of," Conroy said. "You haven't got anything worth listening to."

"What do you think?" I said to Ann.

Still staring emptily at nothing, she shook her head.

"You haven't any right," she said without looking up. "Neither of you has any right."

"I can't help you if I don't know what I'm doing," I said. "Tell me what you know."

"I know I love Marvin," she said.

Seated beside her Kiley closed his eyes for a moment and stretched his neck a little.

"Anyone would," I said. "But are you ready to go to jail with him?"

"If I have to."

"How far out of this can we keep her," Kiley said to me.

"Depends how far in she is," I said. "Much of what I said about Conroy could be said about your daughter."

It was a gamble. But Kiley was a smart guy, and very tough, and if he picked up on it maybe we'd have something.

"You're saying if you can't get him you'll get her?" Kiley said.

He got it it. I wanted to go over and sit in his lap.

"Would work either way," I said.

"You said we could work something out."

"We can, with one of them, but not both, and to tell you the truth, Bobby, I don't especially care which one it is. Hell, it works for me if they both go."

Kiley put an arm around his daughter's shoulders. She seemed to contract in a bit on herself when he did it. Her head was still down.

"Honey," Bobby Kiley said. "Tell us what you know."

She shook her head. Kiley looked at Conroy.

"How about you?"

"I have nothing to say."

"For God's sake, man. I've been in criminal law all my life. They've got enough. This guy will get you. I know this guy. You don't. He'll bring you down, and if you don't help her, my daughter will go with you."

Conroy was silent. He looked at me leaning against the door.

"You tell me what I need," I said, "and I can keep her out of it."

"You and I both love her," Kiley said. "We can't let this happen to her."

Conroy walked to the window and stared through it at the shabby cityscape below him. For the first time since we'd come into the room, Ann Kiley raised her head. Her father's arm still around her, she looked at Conroy. He kept looking out the window. Then, as if he could feel her look, he turned back toward us. None of us said anything. He looked at Ann Kiley. After a long moment Conroy nodded his head.

"Okay," he said.

CHAPTER FIFTY-EIGHT

"I didn't kill anybody," Conroy said.

"You just had it done," I said.

"No. That was Shawcross."

"He had it done?"

"Yeah."

The gloss of Conroy's CEO manner was sloughing off rapidly.

"You were just the middleman," I said.

Conroy shrugged. "I worked for Felton Shawcross," he said.

He was sitting on the edge of the hard chair, his forearms on his thighs, his hands clasped between his knees. Ann Kiley, still in the hotel bathrobe, sat on the bed. Bobby Kiley sat beside her.

"We were working a loan-to-value scam on Pequod," Conroy said. "You need me to explain that?"

I looked at Bobby Kiley.

"I know what a loan-to-value scam is," Kiley said.

"Later," I said.

"Good," Conroy said. "Smith didn't like it, but we knew he was gay, and we knew he was hiding it. So we squeezed him."

"Which is how you got to be president of Pequod," I said.

"Yeah. Smith was chairman, but that was just for show. He did what we told him."

"And?" I said.

"And we were making a fucking fortune," Conroy said.

"But?"

"But Smith wouldn't stay squeezed. He finally said if we didn't move on and let go of his bank he'd go to the cops."

"So?"

"So Shawcross had him killed, and rigged it to look like a suicide. But somebody fucked it up."

"Mrs. Smith," I said. "She thought it was suicide and didn't want to forfeit her insurance and decided to make it look like a murder."

"Which it was," Bobby Kiley said.

Conroy shook his head, thinking about it.

"Ain't that great," he said. "And we didn't know why the suicide setup went wrong, but it did and we had to go to plan B."

"Which was to frame Mary Smith for the murder."

"Yeah."

Conroy looked at Ann Kiley again. She looked back at him. Something went on between them for a moment. I waited for it to stop.

Then I said, "What about Amy Peters?"

"That was bad," he said. "She told me she'd talked to you, asked if there was anything going on she should know about. Said she could serve the bank better if she knew what was up so she wouldn't be blindsided."

"Good employee," I said.

"Yeah. She was very career-driven," Conroy said. "I mentioned it to Felton and that was it for her."

"Just for asking?" Ann said.

Conroy looked at her again for a moment.

"Felton is a really smart guy," Conroy said. "But he's . . . he's like Stalin or somebody. Any suspicion, you're dead."

"Must have been fun to work for," I said. "What happened to Brink Tyler."

"I don't know. I mean, I know Felton had him zipped, but I never knew what for. Maybe Smith talked to him about his situation—you know, had a problem related to money, so he talked with his broker? Guys like Smith sometimes don't have anyone else to talk to."

"How about guys like you?" I said.

"I had Ann," he said. "Maybe Tyler decided to cut himself in, whatever. He knew something, so Felton had him killed."

"Who's doing all this killing?" Bobby Kiley said.

"We recruited local guys."

"How?" I said.

"Through DeRosa. They never knew who they were working for."

"Would Shawcross kill someone himself if he had to?" I said.

"Sure."

"DeRosa was a valuable man," I said. "Why waste him on the Mary Smith frame?"

"He was in jail anyway," Conroy said. "Small-time street thing, the asshole. We got it fixed. But meanwhile, it gave him a reason to make a deal with the DA for ratting out Mary Smith."

"Credibility," I said. "Who were the stumblebums that followed me around and tried to brace me in the parking garage?"

"They were from Felton. He had some people on, ah, staff."

"But he didn't use them for heavy lifting?"

"No," Conroy said. "Not usually. He wanted to keep that separate. Anybody who did any killing only knew DeRosa."

"That true of the guys that tried me in Fort Point?"

"Yes."

"Who pulled the trigger on DeRosa?"

"I don't know. Maybe Felton."

"Because I was getting too close?"

"I don't know how close you were getting," Conroy said, "but you wouldn't go away. Killing you hadn't worked, so he had DeRosa killed to cut you off, and he told me to disappear."

"Which you did."

"Yeah."

"Except." I looked at Ann.

Conroy nodded. His voice was heavy. "Yeah," he said. "And you figured it out."

"Why were you checking Smith out at the gay clubs?" I said.

"You know about that, too," Conroy said wearily.

"We never sleep," I said.

"I was trying to figure out what Shawcross had on him. I got some sort of gay hit off him in the bank. All those boys . . . I don't know. I just had a suspicion."

"How did Shawcross know?"

"I don't know."

"The name Roy Levesque mean anything?" I said.

"No."

"Larson Graff?"

"No."

"How about Joey Bucci?" I said.

Conroy frowned. "Bucci?"

"Yeah."

"When I was at the bank we lent him some money."

"You remember all the bank loans?" I said.

"No. This one was no interest, open-ended, you know? A gift. Felton told us to do it."

"You know why?"

Conroy shook his head.

"You know where Shawcross is now?"

"No idea."

"Is that his real name."

"No idea."

"Will he come after you when he knows you're talking like this?" Ann said.

"What fucking difference does it make, Annie?" Conroy said.

Tears formed in Ann Kiley's eyes. Beside her Bobby Kiley's face was pale and bony. He put his hand on his daughter's shoulder. She didn't appear to notice.

"Shawcross has disappeared," I said. "We don't know where he is. We don't even know who he is. He's safe. Reaching back here for Conroy is a risk that doesn't make any sense."

Conroy shrugged.

"We can keep Ann out of it," Kiley said. "He makes a couple of minor adjustments, which we can help him with, Annie's name never has to come up."

"You okay with that?" I said to Conroy.

He nodded.

"You?" Bobby Kiley said to me.

"Yeah," I said. "I'm all right with that."

CHAPTER
FIFTY-NINE

Abner Grove wore a blue polo shirt and tan slacks, loafers with no socks.

"Casual day?" I said.

Grove smiled. "Every day," he said.

I looked at Rita.

"Abner's so good," Rita said, "he can get away with pretty much anything he wants to."

"He married?" I said.

"Sadly yes," Rita said.

Grove waited patiently while we discussed him.

Then he said, "A loan to value is one where the bank assumes all risk. I don't know the details yet of what Soldiers Field and Pequod were doing. It will take years to peel all that away. But here's how an LTV can work."

"LTV?" I said.

"Loan to value," Grove said. There was a hint of scorn in his voice.

"That's right," I said.

Grove frowned for a minute, then went on, as if I hadn't teased him.

"I don't want to keep saying Soldiers Field Development every time," Grove said, "so we'll call them Soldier, and we'll call the bank Pequod. Soldier has some property it wishes, or appears to wish, to develop. It borrows say fifty thousand dollars from Pequod and buys the land. It then flips it."

"That is, sells it back and forth," I said. "With somebody in on the deal."

"Yes. Each time inflating the cost and getting a new loan from Pequod to cover it."

"Doesn't the bank get suspicious?" I said.

"Of course," Grove said. "Finally, let's say, Soldier has now inflated the value of this property to a million dollars, and it's quote un-quote owned by their flipping partner. Soldier goes to Pequod for an ADC loan."

"Which would be?" I said.

"Acquisition, development, and construction. They get a loan to value—which is to say that the loan covers all costs, including fees and even interest on the loan for the first two years. There is no down payment."

"I'm beginning to see how this might work out," I said.

"After a time, Soldier defaults on the loan, government insurance covers the loss, and everybody makes a lot of money."

"Doesn't the government catch on after a while?"

"Sometimes. Sometimes Pequod might sell the loan to a sister institution, which gets it off Pequod's books, so that when it defaults it defaults on the sister bank."

"And what's the sister bank get out of that?" I said.

Grove smiled. "Reciprocity," he said.

I looked at Rita. She was wearing a bright green suit today, long jacket, short shirt. Her hair was gleaming. She was leaning back in her chair with her spectacular legs crossed, one foot swinging gently. Her shoes were black.

"Talk a little about interest rates," Rita said to Grove.

"One of the things a bank will do, obviously, to attract depositors is to pay high interest rates. But if you pay too much interest you can't make a profit."

"You have to charge more interest than you pay," I said.

"There you go," Grove said. "You'll make a banker yet. Pequod paid the highest interest in the area. Significantly higher. Possibly because they were not worried about profit."

"Because they were simply Soldier's vehicle for fraud," I said.

"Yes."

"Would the president of Pequod have to know?"

"Almost certainly," Grove said. "But that said, once you got your own man in there . . ."

"Conroy," I said.

He nodded. "Then, while he would know what was going on, he wouldn't have to be involved. He could just get out of the way and let Conroy run the scam."

"How much money are we talking about?" I said.

Grove shrugged, put his head back, pursed his lips, and thought about it.

"A hundred million dollars would not be out of the question," he said.

Rita said, "Jesus Christ!"

"People have been killed for less," I said.

"Mind you, this is all hypothetical," Grove said. "We may never prove any of it."

"We're not compelled to prove any of it, Ab," Rita said. "We're only on the hook for defending Mary Smith."

"That would be your area," Grove said.

"It would," Rita said.

"You have questions," Grove said, "feel free to call me."

"I'll have questions," I said.

Grove nodded, still with a hint of scorn, and went out.

"Grove know his stuff?" I said.

"He knows everything there is to know about finance law. He knows almost nothing about anything else."

"Turned you down?"

Rita smiled. "Dumb bastard," she said.

Rita and I looked at each other for a moment.

Rita waggled her knees at me.

"Remember that scene with Sharon Stone?" Rita said.

"Don't start with me, Rita. You know how excitable I am."

"I've always wanted to see you excited," she said.

I had nothing really good to say to that so I didn't say anything.

"I guess we've got Mary Smith out of the deep water," I said.

"She did try to conceal a murder," Rita said.

"Well, did she," I said. "She set out to conceal a suicide."

"By pretending it was a murder." Rita smiled. "Which in fact it was," she said. "I think we can reason with Owen Brooks about that."

She swung her foot some more, watching as it moved in a small arc. She smiled at me again.

"You know," she said, "Owen's single again."

"A single DA," I said. "What could be better?"

"You think Mary knew anything about the bank-fraud enterprise?" Rita said. Sex and business were two sides of the same thing to Rita.

"I haven't come across any sign of it," I said.

"The murder was the only overlap."

"Far as I can see, except for Graff . . . !"

"What?" Rita said.

"Graff. Graff is the only person left standing that could connect Shawcross to the bank fraud and the murders."

"What about Conroy?"

"Shawcross thinks Conroy is waiting for him in Wamego, Kansas," I said. "Under another name. In another bank."

"And Graff is connected to them?"

"The bank lent him money, interest-free," I said. "He used his original name, Joey Bucci."

"A gift."

"Yep."

"He did something for Shawcross," Rita said.

"You'd think so."

"And with Conroy, Shawcross assumes, still his partner and already laying groundwork for a new fraud . . ."

"Leaves Graff the only loose end I know about."

Again Rita and I looked at each other.

"I think I better go visit Larson," I said.

"Six people have been killed so far," Rita said.

"Let's see if we can hold it at six," I said.

"Be a little careful," Rita said. "I haven't slept with you yet."

CHAPTER SIXTY

Larson Graff denied that he knew Felton Shawcross, denied that he had introduced Mary Toricelli to Nathan Smith, denied that he had anything to fear, and insisted therefore that he was not afraid. I didn't believe any of it.

"Do me one favor," I said. "If a man named Felton Shawcross, whom you don't know, shows up, or calls and wants to see you, lock your doors and call me."

"That's ridiculous," Graff said.

His face was pale and tight and his mouth moved stiffly when he spoke. I gave him my card.

"Of course it is," I said. "So am I. But if Shawcross or anyone else that you don't know wants to see you, call me."

Graff was silent, sitting in his state-of-the-art swivel chair, behind his big maple desk with the red leather top. His Adam's apple bounced as he swallowed. I stood and walked toward the door. I had my hand on the knob before he spoke.

"He called," Graff said.

I took my hand off the knob and turned, and walked back to Graff's desk and sat back down in the client chair.

"Shawcross?" I said.

"That was the name he said."

"Where does he want to meet you," I said.

A quick flicker of surprise pushed through Graff's look of cold panic for a moment.

"The parking lot at the Blue Hill Trailside Museum."

"In Milton," I said.

"Yes."

"What time?"

"Nine," Graff said. "At night."

"The museum closes about five," I said.

"I guess so."

"So the parking lot will be empty and it'll be dark," I said. "Nothing to worry about there."

"Would you go with me?" Graff said.

The valve had opened, and his resolve was running out.

"Why go at all?" I said.

"I . . . I feel I should."

"A guy you don't even know?"

"Can you go?" Graff said.

"I'll go instead," I said.

"Instead of me?"

"Yes. You lend me your car. He thinks it's you. I jump out and say *ah ha!*"

"Maybe it won't be him," Graff said.

"It'll be him. As I explained so carefully but a few moments ago, you are the only one left, as far as he knows, who can tie him to any of this mess. He isn't going to send somebody to do it, then that person becomes a threat. He's going to do it himself."

"Do it?"

"Kill you," I said.

Graff leaned suddenly forward in his chair as if he had a stomach cramp.

"Oh God," he said.

"Not to worry," I said. Soothing. "I can fix it. All you have to do is tell me what you know, and then I'll handle Shawcross."

"You can't handle him," Graff said. His voice had become squeaky. "Nobody can handle him."

"Tell me what you know," I said.

CHAPTER SIXTY-ONE

The next morning I went to a place on lower Washington Street that sold what it called "novelties," and bought one. In the middle of the afternoon, I took my novelty and followed Larson Graff while he drove his black BMW sedan down to Milton and parked in the museum lot at the foot of the Blue Hill. The lot was maybe two-thirds full and Graff parked at the far end of it, away from the museum, between a Chevy Blazer and a Ford minivan, near the foot of one of the trails leading up into the hill. I parked behind him. He got out. I got out with my novelty and put it on the driver's seat, then Graff and I got in my car and drove in silence back to Boston. Graff had told me everything he knew yesterday morning in his office with fear singing at the edge of everything he said. Neither of us had much more to say today.

In the late afternoon I joined the south-bound commuter traffic and drove back to Milton. I parked on a shoulder on Route 138 about a half mile from the Trailside Museum, took my raincoat from the backseat and carried it with me as I walked on down to the parking lot. I was wearing a replica Boston Braves baseball cap, New Balance running shoes, jeans, a T-shirt, and a Browning 9mm semiautomatic pistol on my belt, with the T-shirt hanging out to be less conspicuous. I had two extra magazines in my hip pocket. There were only three or four cars in the parking lot when I got there. Graff's BMW sat alone at the far end. I paid it no attention and started up one of the paths near the museum. It was hot and gray and the air was dense with the unculminated promise of heavy rain.

I went up the narrow trail for maybe 100 yards, turned left out of sight of the parking lot, and worked my way through the humid woods to a point above where Graff's car was parked. I sat at the base of a large tree, put my back against it, and waited.

The last stragglers from the museum wandered into the parking lot and got in their cars and departed. Finally, Graff's BMW was the only one left. As it grew dark, it grew no cooler. It seemed impossible that the atmosphere could still contain the rain that thickened it. In the woods there was the rustle and movement and sound that woods always seem to have. A few pretentious raindrops plopped onto the leaves in the treetops above me. There would be more. I stood and put on my raincoat. I took the Browning out of its holster and put it into the side pocket of the raincoat before I zipped the coat up. A few more raindrops pattered. The scatter was decreasing. Then they were steady. Then, as if the energy that held them had released, they cascaded joyously. I sat as stolidly as I could. Hunching my shoulders didn't help.

It was hard to see my watch in the wet darkness, but I think it was ten minutes to nine when a car, maybe a Buick, with its headlights on, swung into the parking lot and drove in a circle around the lot before it parked near Graff's BMW. The wipers stopped. The head-lights went out.

I waited.

Nothing else happened. The car sat there three spaces away from the BMW. I stood and began to move through the woods, down the slope, fighting the tendency to slide on the wet hillside. I was almost to the edge of the parking lot when the door of the Buick opened and a piggish man got out. He had a trench coat belted tight and a soft wide-brimmed hat pulled down. He closed the car door and thrust his hands in his pockets and walked to Graff's car. I was in the parking lot now, on the other side of the Buick away from the man and the BMW. I had the Browning out, and held it pointed down by my leg as I walked. I didn't want the barrel to fill with rainwater. Whatever front had brought the rain with it was colliding with the front that had made it hot. Lightning appeared and thunder followed. The rain was hard and steady. Soon, there'd probably be a plague of locusts.

The man in the trench coat reached the side of Graff's BMW and without pausing opened the driver's side door with his left hand, took his right hand out of his pocket, and shot into the car as fast as he could pull the trigger, too fast for a clear count of the shots. Eight or ten was the best I could do. Then silence, the shots mixing with the thunderstorm and fading into the rain. I thought about DeRosa and his girlfriend, shot to pieces, but by someone who must have liked the work. With the car door open the interior light had come on. The man leaned in and looked at what was left of what he'd shot.

From the other side of the Buick, I said, "Nice shooting."

The man reared up out of the driver's side. As he did he took a second gun out of his left-hand pocket. It was bigger than the one in his right. The man was Shawcross.

"You just murdered a twenty-eight-dollar Inflate-a-mate," I said.

He raised the gun in his right hand. I ducked behind the Buick. He fired and missed. Lightning jagged brilliantly above us and the thunder followed hard upon. Shawcross fired again and moved toward the back of the Buick. As he did, I moved toward the front. We were like the two legs of a carpenter's compass. I stayed now, near the front, listening hard. I was aware of his movement at the other end of the car, but I couldn't exactly see him. I could feel the charge in my nerve endings. My breathing was quick and shallow. I thought about how long we could circle the car like this in the thunderous downpour. I thought about dropping to the ground and shooting under the car at his feet. But it was a hell of a shot in the darkness, and if I missed it left me vulnerable to return fire, being flat down on the ground.

Straining hard I thought I could hear his feet shift on the gravel. He had a lot of shots left: five or six more in the nine, a full magazine in the other gun—which might have been a .45. I crouched at my end of the Buick, keeping myself behind the right front wheel in case he tried a shoot-the-foot trick. I was thinking so hard about Shawcross that I didn't know anymore that it was raining. The thunder and lightning disappeared, too, and all there was was the vibrating connective between us, at either end of the car. I could hear his breath, quick and shallow, too. He jumped suddenly to one side and fired three more rounds from the nine. He was firing into the dark where he hoped I might be. Which was silly. Again nothing moved. Shawcross on his side, me on mine, just another kind of outdoor game. I thought about DeRosa again. With the storm blocked out and Shawcross crouching motionless at his end of the car, I felt as if I were encased in a crystal silence. I thought about Amy Peters. Enough!

I stepped back a little from the front of the car, got a running start, jumped up on the hood of the Buick. Two steps to the roof. On the roof. Shot straight down at Shawcross. Four shots. Point-blank. He was probably dead before the second round went in. I stood on the roof of the car looking down at him and felt the rain again. And saw the lightning. And heard the thunder.

"You son of a bitch," I said.

CHAPTER SIXTY-TWO

Susan and I had been making love with one another for quite a number of years now, and had gotten quite expert. I liked to think that it was that Susan had learned everything from the Grand Master but was forced to admit that she had been married to somebody else, once. And there had been the odd gap in our relationship some years back that had given both of us an opportunity for research. Still, I felt I could claim a lot of credit.

"You know," I said after a particularly successful encounter, "you never say thank you."

"For showing me a good time?"

"Well, yes."

"Gee," Susan said with her head against my shoulder. "I was sort of proud of my own contribution."

"Which was not inconsiderable," I said.

"And which may never be made again if this conversation continues."

We were quiet. Pearl was old enough and deaf enough so that she could be asked to lie on the floor during these encounters and would do so without curiosity. Now, however, when we were in, as it were, phase two, she had gotten herself up slowly and was standing by the bed with her nose two inches from my ear, waiting to be boosted up. I rolled off the bed and boosted her up. She turned several times around and settled arthritically in between us with a big sigh.

"This makes postcoital snuggling something of a problem," I said.

"Thank God," Susan said. But she slid her hand under Pearl's neck and rested it on top of mine.

"So, how 'bout them Sox," I said.

"Would you like to debrief," Susan said, "about the Smith business."

"Larson Graff was so grateful that I took Shawcross out for him that he told me more than I ever wanted to know."

"He did put Smith and his wife together?"

"Yes. He knew Mary from high school. He knew Smith from the closet. He knew Smith needed a beard, and he knew Mary was stupid and avaricious. So was her boyfriend, so the three of them figured out that she could be Smith's beard, continue to see Levesque, and among them skim some of Smith's money. Unfortunately they came head-to-head, unfortunate phrase, with some people more avaricious, less stupid, and much more brutal, who were after the same thing."

"Shawcross and company."

"Yep. Shawcross was looking for a banker to squeeze and Larson Graff knew it and supplied Smith."

"Closet boy."

"Yeah."

"How did Shawcross know Graff?"

"Graff did some legitimate publicity party work for Shawcross after Shawcross came to town and was establishing his legitimacy."

"Did Shawcross kill Nathan Smith?"

"Did or had it done."

"And the others?"

"Same answer. He apparently killed DeRosa and his girlfriend personally. The guns he had with him when I shot him are the same guns that killed them."

Lying on her back Susan put one leg up in the air and straightened it like a ballet dancer and looked at it. I looked at it, too.

"According to Rita's financial guy a scheme like the one that Shawcross was running on Pequod Bank was good for maybe a hundred million dollars."

Susan was still looking at her leg.

"Would you pay that much to see me naked?" Susan said.

"I don't have to," I said. "But it is money that a lot of people would kill for and Shawcross was one of them. Conroy, too, I guess, though I don't think he actually pulled a trigger."

"Maybe I should charge," Susan said.

"Per view?" I said.

"Un-huh."

"Can I run a tab?" I said.

She put her leg down and turned her head and smiled at me.

"Yes, you can," she said.

Susan drew a small circle with her fingertips on the back of my hand.

"So what will happen to them?" she said.

"Mary Smith and Levesque have probably done more crime than we know. But, based on what we know, I doubt that either of them will do any time. Conroy's going to jail."

"That's sort of too bad."

"That's just sentimental," I said. "He was part of a scheme that got half a dozen people killed."

"Yes, but Ann Kiley loved him and he loved her enough to get himself caught."

"Ann who?"

"Kiley," Susan said and paused. "Oh," she said. "You're going to keep her out of it."

"Yes."

"Because she loved not wisely but too well?"

"Yeah. That's one thing."

"What else?" Susan said.

"Her father loves her," I said.

Susan looked at me for a while. I looked back. It was like looking into my own soul.

"Now who's sentimental," she said.

I nodded.

"Do you think we could get Pearl to move?" I said.

"Sure," Susan said. "I'll bribe her with a cookie."

"Okay."

Susan got up, elegantly stark naked, and went to the kitchen and returned with a dog biscuit, which she waved under Pearl's nose. Pearl perked, and tracked the cookie to the foot of the bed, where Susan helped her down. She settled onto the floor with her cookie and Susan jumped back onto the bed.

"Now what?"

"I owe you about a thousand dollars' worth of nude looks," I said.

"Maybe we can work out a payment schedule."

"I could maybe bop your rear molars out," I said.

Susan smiled at me. "Well," she said, "since you put it so nicely."

Surprisingly, her molars remained stable . . . though I think they might have loosened a little.